NO PEACE FOR THE DAMNED

Printed in the United States of America.

Published by 47North
P.O. Box 400818
Las Vegas, NV 89140

ISBN-13: 9781612183602
ISBN-10: 1612183603

NO PEACE FOR THE DAMNED

MEGAN POWELL

TO BRIAN

PROLOGUE

Escape. The word never even occurred to me until tonight.

I hesitated just inside the tree line to catch my breath, looked back toward the estate's main house, and listened for any sign that I had been discovered.

There was nothing.

Just the high wall circling the estate, with its large white stones and black bricks looming ahead of me, more ominous than ever under the night's starless sky.

Grandmother would have been *so* proud.

I scanned the woods around me. In the shadows, I easily located the tiny red light of the security camera between the branches of an adult fir tree.

On a silent inhale, I stretched out my power until I was completely invisible. I took a hesitant step forward. The camera turned in my direction, paused, then returned to its base position. No alarms sounded in the distance.

I released a shaky breath and focused again on the shining wall in front of me. Freedom was only a few feet away. Whatever the outside world held, it had to be better than here. I *needed* it to be. I needed no more blood or broken bones. No more snarls and midnight attacks.

But could I ever fit into a world without those things?

A sound came from behind me. Leaves rustled, debris crunched. My breath caught in my throat. I glared at the wall.

In a single stride I sprang forward, bounding over the wall, landing silently on the balls of my feet. I was moving before my heels even touched the ground.

I felt weightless, my legs no longer running but dancing over the cold earth. I could practically feel the clinging chains of my father falling from my body, recoiling into the glistening wall of his created hell.

I ran until I hit pavement. The highway. My breath caught, and I skidded to a halt on the smooth surface. The smell of asphalt under my feet, the wind, the night, the sounds of small creatures and insects who lived in the brush all registered perfectly in my mind. But that was all.

There was no stench of the guards who whispered angrily at their stations. No violent cries from my uncle's adversaries in the throes of his interrogation. No plots from my father or brothers to force my mind alert.

There was nothing.

A sob tore from my chest—a sound more laughter than lament. My fingers gently brushed along the smooth line of healed flesh that stretched the circumference of my neck.

I *was* free.

My knees crashed hard to the road. My head fell into the cradle of my invisible hands. I cried in joy, in release, in fear. I cried, and let the tears consume me.

By the time I opened my eyes to the speeding headlights it was too late. The vehicle plowed into me, the front tires crushing both my pelvis and my skull, dragging me with its undercarriage until it screeched to a stop.

In that last moment of consciousness I had to chastise myself. I was not supposed to live in this world without violence and pain. And I was an idiot to have ever let myself think otherwise.

There was no peace for the damned.

CHAPTER 1

Lying down on the narrow bench wasn't the most comfortable way to pass the morning, but at least I was hidden enough to avoid stares—and I had a whiskey to sip. I had to give the Network guys credit—this place really was a perfect front. Peanut shells scattered across the floor, Mellencamp crooning on the jukebox, tenderloin lunch special wafting in the air—no one walking into the Thirsty Turtle would ever think *secret meeting place for plotting against supernatural terrorists.*

They might think *tetanus shot,* but whatever.

Movement across the room grabbed my attention. An old drunk had been sitting at the bar since before Thirteen headed downstairs. Smelly and filthy, the man sat hunched on a barstool, slurring his words as he talked to himself. His voice was low and the place was crowded, so I honed in to hear his mumbles. "Downstairs? Down where? Goin' on a hunt for Miller's secret breading? Well, I can tell you it ain't in the Turtle's basement, that's for sure. Miller has his secrets locked up somewhere else. Ain't no one touching this man's special spices."

It was total gibberish, but still. Miller's secrets? He had no idea. I lifted my head and took a long drink. I should just leave. Run away and never look back. My family thought I was really dead—they wouldn't be coming for me. I still had time…

My cell phone chirped, and I jumped. I still wasn't used to the stupid thing. I pulled it out, glanced at the text message from Thirteen. No words, just a smiley face—one with a semicolon for the eyes so it looked like it was winking. I chuckled before I could stop myself.

Crap. I wasn't going anywhere.

Two guys pushed through the bar's front doors. *OK, here we go.* Just like I had with the other members of Thirteen's special team, I did a quick mental peek at each of them. The first thing I noticed: Jon Heldamo's mind was far too easy to access for a Network leader. Oh, he wasn't a chief like Thirteen or anything, but he wanted to be. Someday. He was smart, skilled, and he already walked with that arrogant gait that Thirteen had mastered. On Thirteen it was endearing. On Jon it was just annoying.

Jon wasn't the one who worried me, though. I shifted in my seat as an uneasiness settled low in my stomach. *Theo Mahle.* Yeah, something was definitely up with this second guy.

According to Jon, Theo didn't give a shit about being a Network chief. He, too, was smart and well-trained—maybe even more than Jon—and Theo's mental shields were solid. I could still get through them, but it would take a strong push. He walked two steps behind Jon, guarding his partner's back just like Banks always did for Thirteen.

I struggled against the urge to sit up and get a good look when Jon's scent suddenly hit me. Polo cologne. Shit. My fists clenched as Malcolm's face flashed in my mind. His cover-model features and soulless eyes—just like Father's. The sharp tang of the cologne filling my nose, his hot, eager breath on my face. The pain. I'd try not to hate Jon for it, but God, it would be hard. The thought of spending the upcoming weeks smelling that crap again and again…

Jon's cologne faded just as Theo's smell hit me like a punch. My stomach tightened. My chest grew warm. *Whoa.* Musk, metal, male—I'd never smelled anything so—so intoxicating.

What the hell? I caught myself. I was *never* affected by anyone like this.

I gripped my whiskey and stayed low on my bench. The door to the kitchen swung shut. Jon's and Theo's footsteps echoed on the back stairs, heading down to the meeting room where my introduction would take place. I listened carefully as they entered the large basement conference room. The hum of the room's security system paused as they opened the door. Thirteen had told me the room was impenetrable to psychic eavesdropping. I don't know what contractor sold him that load of bull, because I could hear all ten team members just fine. And not just the murmured speculations about the meeting's purpose, or the click-clacking of some guy named Chang on his laptop. Their thoughts were as crystal clear as the stressed businessmen's in the booth next to me.

I clinked my ring on the side of my glass to get a refill. Miller stomped up to my booth and slammed the bottle of whiskey on the table. He loomed over me even as he kept his eyes off my face.

"Just keep the damn bottle, why don't ya," he growled. I just sighed and jiggled the ice in my glass. Miller huffed and grumbled, then pulled out a clean glass he just happened to have behind his back. It already held ice and sour mix. I smiled. He could deny it all he wanted, but Miller liked me.

He poured my drink then hurried back to the bar, the whiskey bottle gripped tight in his hand. His thoughts stumbled as he made his way across the room. Images raced through his mind: my thick, dark hair, my long legs bent on the booth bench. Thirteen had made me wear these ridiculous capri pants in an effort to appear more conservative. I thought I looked like an idiot, but Miller had no problem at all with the way my annoying pants hugged the curves of my legs.

Miller wouldn't be in the meeting today. Aside from running the Turtle, I wasn't sure what role he actually played. I'd have to ask Thirteen later on.

"If everyone will have a seat, we'll get started."

Thirteen's quiet command brought the underground meeting to attention. I'd gotten so attuned to him over the last couple of months I didn't even have to concentrate to hear him from below.

"We have a new source. As this task force was created to focus specifically on the activities of the Kelch brothers, you can be certain that the knowledge provided by this individual will be directly related to the family. You each know just how important accurate information is whenever dealing with a supernatural threat. It's even more important when it comes to the Kelch family. With that in mind, this source's information has been deemed valuable enough to assign temporary agent status as a consulting member of this task force."

Their thoughts swirled with anticipation. My stomach knotted again.

"But first," Thirteen continued, "Banks? A status update, please."

Banks's mechanical leg whined as he pushed himself to standing. Why the big man insisted on looking like a cyborg rather than getting himself proper prostheses was beyond me. There was a soft scrape of metal on metal as he rubbed his thumb ring over the silver eye patch that was sewn directly into his skin. His barking voice shook the conference room. "Two days ago, Harold Meador's body was found and ID'd on Chicago's Red Line. How the local sheriff ended up riding the EL in the Windy City is the least of our worries. Meador is the third Network member's body to be discovered outside city limits. Someone is taking us out."

He paused for dramatic effect, and I rolled my eyes. The sooner his update was over, the sooner I could get my part over with.

"Each of our men was abducted while on assignment, each body found just across state lines. Emme Thewlis was the first, found two weeks ago in a dumpster outside a Steak-n-Shake in Henderson, Kentucky. Zak Inge was found nine days ago sitting in a back booth at Zips Diner in Cincinnati. Thewlis was a customer service manager for the overseas pharmaceutical division of Kelch Incorporated. Inge was a junior aide to a House rep who shared conference room space with Senator Maxwell Kelch. All three bodies were autopsied and found to have died from internal injuries that are right in line with the Kelch way of torture."

I took another long drink. Grinding metal squealed again as Thirteen and Banks broke from the meeting and headed upstairs. Almost time.

I put in my new iPod earplugs and closed my eyes tight. It wasn't enough. The sound of their footfalls still pounded in my ears. Thirteen's presence had physical weight as he slid into the booth bench across from me.

"It's time, Magnolia."

I didn't sit up. "Yeah, I know."

The knot in my stomach upgraded to a full-blown cramp. I didn't want to move. I didn't want to go downstairs and meet these people who were not going to like me and were not going to want to hear what I had to say. Most of all, I didn't want to be a Kelch anymore.

"Never took you for a coward, Magnolia," Banks growled as he put two fresh shots of whiskey on the table. "Didn't think it was in yer blood."

I took a deep breath. I would do this for Thirteen; I owed him that much. I waited until my song was over, then wrapped up my earphones, shoved my iPod in my pocket, and gave in.

As I sat up, my long hair fell forward to cover half my face. Thirteen didn't react at all, but Banks's leg squeaked again as he staggered in place. And Miller's audible gasp from across the room made me want to groan. The man seriously needed to get a grip.

Thirteen leaned forward until I met his eyes. He was enormous. Even sitting, I had to look up to see his face. His gray hair was longer now than it had been the night I'd escaped, and he'd lost some weight recently—probably from stress—but neither change took away from the innate authority that radiated off him. The crinkles around his bright blue eyes softened. God, the look on his face—such an odd mixture of pride and worry. No one had ever looked at me the way he did.

With a slight nod to one another, we stood. I paused long enough to throw back one of Banks's offered shots then followed the two men through the kitchen door. The back stairs were longer than I thought, and at the bottom a tall, light-haired woman stood in front of the auto-locked metal door that led to the meeting room. She was attractive enough—midtwenties with high cheekbones and a thin frame—but her eyes were too sharp to be pretty. She casually looked over my outfit, pretending to admire my clothes while really looking for weapons. Then she met my gaze. And gasped. Just like Miller, her mind drifted into a lust-filled stupor.

"Ugh! See?" I motioned to the woman. "I told you this would happen."

Thirteen patted my arm. "Cordele," he said coolly.

She blinked. Then blinked again. Finally, she shook herself, opened the door, and stepped aside, glaring at me the whole time.

I didn't move until she walked back toward the long meeting table in the center of the room. She didn't know what I had just done to her, but she knew it was some kind of power. And she was pissed.

Great. I hadn't even entered the room and already one of my "teammates" hated me.

Chapter 2

Theo sat at the head of the table beside Jon. His scent had drawn me like a magnet the moment I walked in the room. He was gorgeous: a jaw rough with stubble, long hair that curled at his collar, eyes warm like melted chocolate. The hard contours of his face put my brothers' pretty-boy looks to shame. And when he gasped at the sight of me, sucking in a deep breath along with everyone else in the room, his faded T-shirt stretched tight over his muscled chest, my own breath faltered. Power pulsed beneath my skin. This was wrong. I was too distracted. Vulnerable.

I dragged my gaze away from him and forced myself to focus on the nine other people in the room. Banks and Thirteen stood off to the side. Most everyone had blinked themselves back into focus and were now either confused or pissed. The GI Joe seated closest to me, a big guy named Charles Hilliby, was especially itching for a fight. As was his wife, Marie, the Latina fashionista to his right. Their minds were sharp, suspicious, but neither of them was really a concern. Not like the psychic I sensed in the room. Automatically, I made sure my mental walls were set.

A loud smack came from my side, and I turned. Banks had whopped the small Asian techno-geek, Nicky Chang, on the back of his head. Chang coughed and sputtered, then covered his eyes with his hands—like if he didn't see me, maybe I'd just go away. I rolled my eyes. Only the weakest minds got so out of whack at the sight of me that they had to be slapped back into focus.

"Er, we're sorry about that." A pretty brunette rose from her seat on the opposite side of the table. "We just weren't expecting…well, someone like you. You know, with powers."

We wore nearly identical outfits, only she looked comfortable in hers. Then she smiled. "I'm Heather," she said brightly, "Heather Lamping. Welcome to the team."

What. The hell. Was this?

Thirteen's team was supposed to be an elite task force. An experienced group of Network agents willing to take down my father and uncles. Instead, he had trigger-happy newlyweds, a video gamer who couldn't look at me without passing out, and a fucking preschool teacher complete with patient smile and peach sweater set. Hell, other than Theo and Jon—who were dangerously controlled at the moment—the only other capable fighters at the table seemed to be that chick Cordele who'd opened the door and a silent blond giant named Shane Bailey. He hadn't missed a thing since I'd walked in. I turned to Thirteen, the angry confusion plain on my face.

Look closer, his thoughts whispered. He'd lowered his mental shields, anticipating my telepathy. I glared at him for a moment then turned back toward Heather. She smiled expectantly.

"Um, hi," I finally managed. Her smile turned sympathetic as she sat back down. I probed deeper into her mind. She had strong, natural mental blocks like Theo, but they were easily pushed aside.

God, her thoughts were as pleasant as her smile. Genuine, kind, sympathetic…wait a minute. Not sympathetic. Empathetic. She actually related to what it was like for me to stand here, knowing that everyone in the room was suspicious of me. She felt it as if it were her own discomfort. She was the psychic I'd felt earlier. But she was more than that. She was a true empath.

And she had absolutely no idea.

I turned wide eyes to Thirteen. I could block psychic intrusions, no problem. But an empath? I didn't want this lady knowing my feelings all the time. *What the hell, Thirteen?* He ignored my silent question and stepped forward again.

"I would like to introduce you to our newest team member," Thirteen said evenly. "Magnolia Kelch."

Jaws dropped, faces blanched. Shock and anger permeated the room. But Theo and Jon showed nothing. No reaction, no movement. Just total control. If those two turned out to be as strong as I sensed they were, maybe Thirteen didn't need the rest of the team.

GI Joe Charles swung around in his chair and grabbed my wrist. "How dare you bring an enemy…!"

I didn't think. I just reacted.

I crushed his hand instantly, the bones breaking to bits under my grip. I slammed a quick extended-knuckle fist into his larynx, no more than bruising his windpipe, but incapacitating him nonetheless. Then I swung him completely out of his chair, twisting him to his knees in front of me, his back pressed to my front, his broken-handed arm pinning him in place. The Glock 34 he'd had tucked into the waistband of his jeans now rested nicely in my other hand. I pressed the gun to his temple.

Everyone leaped to their feet, guns out, all pointed at me. Charles gurgled and I pressed the gun tighter to his forehead. Thirteen waved his arms in the air yelling something like, "Don't!" or "Stop!"

"Magnolia…" Banks said, as if trying to reason with me. But he didn't lower his gun.

"Lower your weapons!" Thirteen commanded. No one moved. "Lower your weapons! NOW!"

All guns pointed to the floor. *C'mon Thirteen, don't be a buzz kill. Let's see what they're really made of.* His stare bored into the side of my face.

"That means you too, Magnolia."

At a normal speed, I released Charles and lowered his gun to my side. I watched with amusement as he scurried across the floor to Marie. Well, that had been fun. I turned to Thirteen and my amusement evaporated. He sighed deeply, his thoughts full of disappointment and regret. Damn it, it wasn't my fault that Charles guy had grabbed at me.

"Heather," Thirteen said, "please run upstairs and get some ice and a first aid kit from Miller." Heather didn't look at me as she rushed to the door.

"Please," Thirteen continued. "Please, everyone just find your seats and let's start again."

I took my place beside him, leaning against the wall.

"Magnolia is here to help us," Thirteen began again. "She can very obviously handle herself, but more importantly, she is offering her insight, her knowledge. And she is offering this at great personal risk and sacrifice."

Thirteen looked each person in the eye before he turned a softer gaze to me. The disappointment was gone, replaced by a warm reassurance. How could he make me feel so accepted with just one look? Even after I'd just injured one of his agents? Shit. I was *way* too close to Thirteen.

When Heather returned, she wrapped Charles's hand in a makeshift splint and an Ace bandage. "Be careful," he hissed between clenched teeth as she finished taping him up.

I could heal him. It would be painful, considering how many bones were broken in his hand, but I could still do it. He glared at me over his shoulder. Maybe I'd offer later.

"Magnolia is here to share her insight," Thirteen explained again, trying to get the meeting back on track. "And just to give you an idea of how valuable that insight is, she has agreed to a demonstration."

"Haven't we already had a demonstration?" Theo asked, getting comfortable again in his seat. "I think we can all agree that the whole take-Charles-down-in-a-blink-of-an-eye thing was proof enough that she is who she says she is."

"Not to mention that we already knew that Kelches could kill with merciless efficiency and unnatural speed," Shane added. It was the first I'd heard him speak. Considering the way his words oozed with malice and hatred, I kinda hoped he'd go back to being the strong, silent one of the group.

Jon leaned forward on the table, his hard stare locked on me. "We need to know why she's here in the first place."

I stepped forward, power already rising under my skin. Thirteen touched a hand to my arm, stopping me. He had had this whole explanation planned for the group: how I would use a power they'd never seen before to project a memory of my family into their minds, providing real-life footage of my family's abilities. He'd been so eager for them to see what a valuable resource I'd be that he'd forgotten the most important thing about me: I was a Kelch. Charles's jumping the gun and now Jon's questioning my motives brought him back to reality.

Thirteen looked at me, then without a word, stepped back, offering me the floor. Guess we'd do the explanation thing later. Resigned, I closed my eyes and reached out with my power, pushing past Heather's and Theo's blocks, until I was deep within the mind of every person in the room. They might have tackled supernatural beings in the past, but they had no clue what horrors awaited them when it came to my family.

It was about time they found out.

CHAPTER 3

Thick leather restraints dug into my wrists and ankles, holding me tight to the metal chair. The chair itself was large, heavy, and bolted to the floor of an otherwise empty tank. I took a deep breath and blinked my eyes into focus.

Cold steel surrounded me, the tank walls gray except where the bolted seams had rusted to a flaky red and green. My legs weren't long enough yet to bend where the seat ended. Instead, my bare feet dangled oddly off the edge, pulling against the straps that held them in place.

Five feet above me, the top of the tank was open. I could see my father's head and shoulders. Dressed in his CEO best, he rested his arms on the tank's edge. He looked down at me, his face pinched in frustration. The water wasn't working right. It was coming out more as a spray than in droplets. It needed to be as close to real rain as possible. I shivered, wearing nothing but panties and an undershirt.

Father's features contorted in disgust the moment our eyes met. He rolled his gaze away from mine and spoke directly to the man next to him. One of my uncles? Probably, but my eyes were still blurred, and I couldn't tell which one. They shared the same dark hair, sculpted features. Their faces all ran together for me.

I turned my head, but the movement tore open a wound on the side of my neck—a soldered gash that went from behind my right ear, down my neck, all the way to my collarbone. It hurt like hell. I knew it was fresh because it had barely started to heal. I could usually heal burns and cuts, even severe ones, in a matter of minutes. That was why Father had taken Uncle Max's advice and started using the soldering irons—to see if the combination of deep tissue tears and flesh-melting burns took longer for me to repair.

"Yes, yes, that should work." The excitement in Father's voice startled me. My stomach automatically lurched. If he was happy, it meant that whatever new means of torture he had been working to perfect was about to be tested. On me.

Father looked down on me again, watching me. The sadistic anticipation on his face made bile rise in my throat. I swallowed it down and braced myself. Four other faces appeared around him, and I now recognized each of my brothers and uncles. Even Uncle Max was there. The feeling of dread quadrupled. Uncle Max was busy these days. He would only have taken the time to watch if it was going to be especially horrific.

My brother Malcolm, now at Father's side, handed him a clunky remote control. Malcolm looked down on me with a gleam in his eye that matched Father's exactly. Markus was sandwiched between my uncles. I didn't have to read his mind to know that he was just happy it wasn't him in the tank. Our eyes met for only a moment before he looked away. Such a coward.

Uncle Max looked at his watch. "I have a meeting at four," he drawled. Father scowled at him.

"You're not going to want to miss this," he said. "Trust me."

All eyes were on me again. I held my breath. Father pushed a large yellow button on the remote. Water sprinkled down on me. I flinched when the first drop touched my skin. Father's deep chuckles from above echoed in the tank around me.

The drops of water sped up as Father made adjustments on his remote. It felt like real rain now—a fast, sharp rain that stung a little with impact. Uncle Max yawned.

Then Father handed the remote back to Malcolm. His face went eerily blank. His eyes dilated so completely that any color his irises had was lost behind the empty ink of his pupils. His skin tightened. His features went completely devoid of emotion. His mask was complete.

This is it.

The sharp coolness of the downpour mutated into a burning wetness. A spasm of screams wrenched from my chest. My eyes clamped shut. Pain pierced through my senses. Like my entire body was being peeled away, one fiery piece of flesh at a time.

The fire rain remained clear, looking every bit as normal as a spring shower. But as the liquid made contact with my skin, it instantly scorched circles into the flesh. Each burn spread, deeper and wider, until the edges of one burn wound met with another. Within minutes I could see cartilage where the liquid burrowed past flesh and muscle.

And the tank was starting to fill. I could no longer hear my own screams. My feet were nearly covered in the pool of acidic rain. The flesh melted away, exposing tendons and bone. And when I looked down, thick chunks of my face fell into my lap. My lungs stopped working; the burning broke through my chest. In one final act of defiance, I forced my melting eyes to my father. Encompassing pleasure spread across his face. Then everything went dark.

It was like changing the channel on a TV show. I switched off the memory and was back in the Thirsty Turtle's basement conference room. It only took me a moment to get my bearings. The others had a more difficult time.

Heather and Cordele struggled to find their breath. Tears streamed down both their faces. Charles huddled in a tight embrace with Marie, trembling. Chang was curled up in the fetal position on the floor, his chair knocked backward. Banks and Shane both had their faces covered with their hands, shaking in restrained sobs.

Jon was the first to move. He scrambled from the head of the table to Heather's seat and pulled her into his lap as she curled in a ball. Her knees tight against her chest, he rocked her back and forth, gently rubbing her back. Then he buried his face in her hair just as she buried her face into his neck.

Wait a minute. *What the hell was this?* This softness, this comfort…this didn't correlate at all with my earlier assessment of Jon. I turned to Theo. He was already staring at me, his brow furrowed with pain and anger. I took a step toward him. His breath hitched and his chin lifted in response, stopping me midstride. *What was I doing?*

"I asked Magnolia to share this memory," Thirteen said in a shaky voice, "to show just what this family is capable of. Experiments such as this one are confirmation that the Kelch brothers have been honing their powers for years. We have to assume they are planning something big."

I stared at the floor, my cheeks burning in humiliation. What Thirteen hadn't said, but what was in the back of everyone's mind, was that no one had ever imagined that the Kelch family would practice their horrible, torturous methods on one of their own.

Always knew they'd kill anyone in their path, Shane thought. *Callous bastards.*

Fucking monsters, Marie silently growled at me. *And she's one of them…*

That guy in Buenos Aires was telepathic, but I've never heard of anyone who could take over our thoughts like that. I glanced over to Jon. *She could completely manipulate our minds if she wanted to.*

Cordele thought I was a mole, here to gain inside information about the Network. Shane and Charles thought I was the perfect distraction, sent by my father to plant false intel, steering the Network away from whatever huge terrorist plot they were concocting. They had visions of my Uncle Max forcing foreign nations into signing contracts, or my father destroying one of the primary competitors of Kelch Incorporated. Whatever was being plotted, it must be huge to send me into enemy hands.

I tried not to roll my eyes.

As if my family thought that much of the Network. Sure, they caused a setback every now and then, but truth be told, the organization was little more than an annoyance to my father. And Senator Max? He thought they were cute.

"Another team needs to use the safe house where Magnolia has been staying," Thirteen said. "So I will be taking her to the southwest HQ where she will be living for the rest of the summer. There is much to be discussed. Take the rest of today to do what you must then we'll meet again at HQ tomorrow evening at six. Until then…" Thirteen wanted to say more, but what was there to say? *Your newest team member just totally mind-fucked you, but really, trust her—she's on our side. And by the way, be nice and don't attack her again. She really doesn't want to have to kill you.*

Yeah, there was nothing else to say.

I turned to leave with Thirteen but glanced back at Theo once more. He hadn't moved since I had pulled back the memory. He knew I was the biggest threat any of them had ever seen. He knew the Network was in over their heads with my family. Any other time, he would have made the practical decision and killed me before it was too late. But this time, with me, the thought of hurting me made him sick. And the thought of someone else hurting me? He reached for the blade hidden at his ankle before he even knew what he was doing.

Our eyes met. His pulse sped until it beat in time with my own. He leaned forward in his seat and gripped the table to hold himself in place just as I gripped the frame of the door.

Thirteen touched my arm and I jumped. *Shit.*

Without looking back, I hurried past Thirteen and out of the room. I didn't breathe again until the metal door was shut securely.

The Network wasn't the only one in over its head.

CHAPTER 4

I loved downtown Indianapolis. The city was alive, vibrating with people. Renovations were everywhere: the Circle Center mall, the convention center, the historic circled street that anchored the city. And with Lucas Oil Stadium having just hosted the Super Bowl, the place was busier than ever. It was awesome, exciting, and I loved it whenever Thirteen brought me here.

Unfortunately, the Network's southwest headquarters were *not* downtown. Not even close.

I followed Thirteen's car nearly fifteen miles before turning off the highway. The occasional cookie-cutter neighborhood sprouted up to separate one long cornfield from the next, but that was it. Eventually we were so far out that the faded green street signs no longer posted street names, only county grid numbers. We turned from E 450 to S 900, and then onto a road that didn't even have a number to post.

Masses of spindly weeds covered the uncultivated land. Thirteen's car turned sharply. *Crap! Was he driving into that field?* Then I saw the imprinted path. Tractors might have ridden on the trail just fine, but there was no way my week-old BMW was going to survive this. The steering wheel jerked as I dipped into the field. *Shit!*

The trail disappeared into the cover of woods at the edge of the field. From the jerks of the tires I figured we were on gravel now. Off in the distance, between the thinning trees, I caught the gleam of white siding.

The gravel trail snaked past a thick grouping of fir trees, and I could make out a clearing up ahead. Thin grass stretched in a nice open yard before the small home in the distance. It looked pleasant. Quaint.

I imagined driving up to my family's estate. Past the guards and the glowing stone wall, the main house would shine with its golden bricks and enormous windows. The home was stunning. Just thinking about it made my stomach roll.

I parked in the grass next to Thirteen's SUV and watched as he and Banks walked toward the front porch. I turned off the engine but didn't move. Up close, I could see that the chipped clay roof tiles had run and stained the worn siding. Someone, probably Thirteen, had put a pot of perennials on the cement steps leading up to the wraparound porch, no doubt trying to make it more welcoming.

It wasn't much at all. But it was mine.

Shane had been the one to donate the old farmhouse to the Network, as well as the nearly three hundred acres surrounding it. It had been left to him a couple of years ago, after his parents died. I knew from Thirteen that it was just one of several private donations that helped keep the Network staffed and operational over the years.

I peeled myself from the car and hauled out my black backpack from the backseat. I threw the bag over my shoulder and walked the broken stone path around to the front of the house.

Banks winked at me as he held open the metal screen door. I stepped past him into the tight entryway. A large great room ran the length of the house to my left, furnished with a couple of tattered, oversized couches and several worn ottomans. The far end of the great room opened into the kitchen, complete with yellow flowered wallpaper and cobwebs that had been there since disco. A thick wooden table was centered in the small room, making it nearly impossible to walk through. Off the kitchen, a narrow corridor led to the only bedroom in the house. A tiny full bathroom, a back door to the rear acres, and a narrow stair to the second story loft completed the home. There was no basement.

I looked out the tiny window over the kitchen sink. The sun shone brightly in my eyes until I had to turn away. Curtains. After I doused the whole place in bleach, I'd have to get new curtains for the little window. And maybe some for the windows in the great room, too. Nice curtains. Yellow ones. And maybe a throw pillow. Nothing with fringe and tassels like the ones on every freaking sofa at the estate. But cute ones. With flowers. Slowly, I felt a smile tug at my lips. Wonder if the bedroom needed curtains too?

Thirteen and Banks talked quietly in the kitchen while I explored.

"…should have the rest of the report by next week. I want you on the call when it arrives so we can make a decision and get everyone moving as quickly as possible. Assuming, of course, it gives us information to move on. I just hope it's not too late."

I walked back to the kitchen, and Thirteen turned to me and smiled. "Not a lot to it, but it's safe and it's yours."

"For now," Banks added with a sideways glance at Thirteen.

I took the key from Thirteen. "Who else has a key?"

He thought about that a minute. "Jon and Theo each have one. They've met informants here in the past."

"Do you have a key?" I asked Banks pointedly.

He narrowed his gaze but said nothing.

Thirteen said, "If you have a key, please give it to her. This is her home now. It would be an invasion of privacy for anyone else to have unfettered access."

Without taking his eyes from me, Banks reached into his back pocket and pulled out a large circle key ring with more keys than I could count. *How in the hell did he ever sit comfortably with a wad of metal like that in his back pocket?*

He moved his fingers swiftly, counting off the keys until he found the right one, then unwound it from the ring.

"Someone else should have a key. A backup," he growled, and slapped the key to my palm. Then he tromped loudly down the corridor from the kitchen and out the back door. The door slammed shut, shaking the cabinet doors.

"If he'd just said he was keeping his key as a backup I would have understood," I admitted to Thirteen. Wouldn't have stopped me from making him hand it over, but I'd have understood his reasoning. "But what the hell was that all about?"

Thirteen's eyes were still on the back door. "With Network members missing, Banks is worried for me, that's all."

But there was more he wasn't saying, and I'd been trying to be less intrusive with Banks and Thirteen in the last couple of weeks. Maybe I needed to rethink that approach.

"I'll try to arrive a little early tomorrow evening. The others were shaken this afternoon, but I know they'll have recovered and be full of questions by the time we meet again. Also, I wanted you to have a bit of time here by yourself. Get to know the place. Get as comfortable as possible before we really begin. Did you see the security monitors in the back?"

"Yeah, I saw them."

"Good. I know I haven't given you a lot of time to get things the way you like, but hopefully it will be enough."

Thirteen looked down at me then, and his face softened. His daughter flashed in his mind. A decade younger than me, she'd only been twelve when Thirteen's enemies had killed her to get to him. It always made my chest swell with emotion whenever he looked at me and saw her.

"I know the place isn't much," he said finally, "but it is, for all practical purposes, yours."

I could be suspicious of everyone else, but Thirteen's motivations rang true for me. He wanted me to feel what the freedom of living here meant. To spread my wings and enjoy my first real taste of independence.

CHAPTER 5

Eighteen seconds. That's how long it took to walk from the front door to the back door of my farmhouse, hitting every room on the way. It had once taken me more than twelve minutes to go from one end of the estate's main house to the other.

I sat at the kitchen table and looked around. The sun was finally setting and shadows were growing longer. I liked that. For so long, I'd lived in the shadows. Or at least tried to.

The far corner of the estate's navy guest room had always had the best shadow. No one had ever thought to look for me there because it was basically out in the open. No furniture or draperies to hide behind—just darkness. That's what made it perfect.

I took a long, slow swallow of whiskey and shut my eyes.

I was back in that room, hearing the footsteps tiptoeing down the hall, trying to sneak up on me. I knew they'd be coming. Their thoughts always gave them away.

I rolled out of the bed and silently moved into the dark corner. I slept in a different guest room every night, but they always found me. They were outside the door now. Malcolm and Markus. At least it wasn't Father again. My ribs still ached after his little session with me the night before. He didn't let the boys watch because it disgusted him to see how they reacted to me now that I was a teenager. But by keeping them away last night, he had guaranteed a visit this morning.

The door creaked open and light from the hallway spilled in behind them, keeping their faces dark.

"Do you see her?" Markus whispered.

"Shut up!" Malcolm hissed, then tried to shut the door. Markus pushed past him until he was all the way in the room. Malcolm growled.

I stood statue-still, not even breathing. Their matching blue eyes strained as they searched the room. Markus was growing his brown hair long, but it still wasn't to the length of Malcolm's dark blond. He didn't have Malcolm's bulk yet either, but it didn't matter.

Their senses weren't as good as mine. They could turn on the lights or open the drapes and find me standing there, but the search was part of the thrill. At least for Malcolm.

"She's not in here," Markus said. Then he picked up a silver letter opener from the desk next to the door. He examined it for a minute then slipped it in his pocket. Damn it. I hadn't seen it there. Now he was armed.

"Oh, she's here all right," Malcolm purred, then he called out in a deep, sing-song voice, "Come out, come out, wherever you are."

Markus chuckled, but it was more nervousness than amusement. Markus was scared of me. He was scared of everyone.

Malcolm snuck around the side of the bed. I would have made a run for it except Markus was still by the door. He wasn't as powerful and certainly wasn't as into this game as Malcolm, but he'd try to take me down if I got too close.

Malcolm leaned back on the bed but kept one foot on the floor. "How about this," he said as he fluffed the pillows behind his head. "I'll give you to the count of three. If you don't show yourself, we'll turn on the light. Not even you can hide from the light."

Actually, I could. I could go completely invisible now. But for some reason, I didn't want anyone to know that yet. And Malcolm's game wasn't enough of a threat to give away my new secret.

"One…two…last chance…"

I didn't move.

"Three."

Markus flipped on the light and I squinted into the sudden glare. My eyes had barely adjusted and Malcolm was there. His body slammed me against the wall. His hands immediately went to my chest, his mouth to my neck. He sucked in the skin between his teeth and squeezed at my breasts hard enough that I cried out. The next moment he was flying backward. He slammed against the armoire on the far side of the room, breaking it with a loud crack.

I crouched and turned to Markus. His eyes were wide, the letter opener clutched so tight in his hand his knuckles were white. I didn't wait for his attack. I sent him backward so hard and fast that when he hit the door it broke from its hinges.

Then Malcolm was back, looming over me. He stood just far enough away that I couldn't reach him without stepping closer. His power bit along my skin, reminding me how much stronger he was becoming. I wouldn't be able to fling him across the room again. His eyes were dark and his thoughts swirled with images of what he wanted to do to me. He smiled and wiped the blood trickling from his mouth with a piece of cloth. A piece of my shirt. I suddenly felt the sting of scratches across my chest where he had clung to my nightshirt when I sent him flying. Shit. This was all foreplay to him.

Suddenly the bedroom door shattered. We both jumped. I shielded myself from the debris then was instantly pinned against *the wall by an invisible force. From the corner of my eye, I could see Malcolm facing the door, standing at attention.*

"What the hell do you think you're doing?" Father roared from the bedroom door. He came into the room, stepping over Markus as if he were a stain on the floor. A frustrated glint twinkled in Malcolm's eye. He wouldn't get to finish his game, but at least I'd be punished for his fun.

I closed my eyes as Father moved across the room. A slap against Malcolm's face made me flinch. Then his hot breath was on me. The muscles around my ribcage clenched as if they knew they'd never get the chance to heal before being broken again.

"Looking for attention again, Magnolia?" he hissed, spittle hitting my cheek as he spoke. "Well, I can give you all the attention you need."

I shook myself back into the farmhouse's kitchen. My pulse slowed and I took another drink. Thirteen had wanted me to have freedom here, but until this moment, I hadn't really known what that meant. He didn't want me running all over town by myself—he was still too worried about my safety for that—but he wanted me to feel the freedom of not being on guard every minute of every day.

Those people from the meeting today didn't think like my brothers. I realized now that I had expected them to. In their thoughts I hadn't found any of the malice or deep hatred that coated Malcolm's mind. Or the fear and anger that haunted Markus. Instead, their thoughts were like Thirteen's—intelligent, aggressive, concerned.

I remembered the way Chang had nearly passed out at the sight of me. And the way Theo had looked at me during our strange moment before I left. Even their lusty reactions to me weren't as repulsive as my brothers'.

By the time I finished my drink, locked the front and back doors, and went back into the bedroom, it was almost dark. I pulled on a T-shirt and slipped into the bed. My bed. My room. My house. No one was going to hurt me here. No one was even going to try. I repeated the words over and over until I finally fell asleep.

Chapter 6

The next morning, I went for a walk. The morning air was fresh with dew. As I wandered through the woods around the farmhouse I thought of Uncle Mallroy. He loved mornings like this. The stillness, the gray landscape. He'd always gotten so upset if someone dared interrupt his morning commune with nature. For once, I understood the feeling.

"You know, it's not polite to follow people," I called out.

Thirteen chuckled. He pushed the branches away and walked to the edge of the woods beside me.

"You're right," he said. "And I apologize. I was just anxious to see you. Did you sleep OK?"

I shrugged. "Well enough."

"Are you ready for this evening's meeting?"

"Yeah, about that—I've been thinking about something you told me a while ago. You said that Network membership is anonymous. But all those people yesterday already knew each other. I thought this special task force was a new thing."

"The task force is new, but the agents I've chosen are experienced. They've worked on previous missions and have crossed paths with one another before. Also, yesterday's meeting wasn't the first the task force has had. It was just the first you've attended."

"I don't know why you don't just list out an employee directory anyway. Seems to me it would be easier if everyone knew who everyone was."

"Everyone knows who is on their assigned team," he explained with a hint of annoyance. "That's all they need to know. The people we track have supernatural abilities, Magnolia, and are extremely dangerous. If the Network or our members became public knowledge…"

"Covers blown, danger to agents' families, blah, blah, blah—I remember the conversation."

He shook his head at me and sighed. "You really surprised them yesterday. Your powers, your aura—they've never seen anything like you." He hesitated. "I think every single one of them called me last night, bombarding me with questions about you." He cleared his throat. "I filled them in as best I could, but some things you'll have to answer yourself. If you're comfortable doing so."

I ground my teeth. "I thought we were past the evasiveness, Thirteen. If you want to know something, just ask."

He stepped in front of me, his wide frame blocking out the rising sun. "Why you, Magnolia?" he asked quietly. "Everyone in your family has powers. Why were you the only one they tortured?"

Humiliation sat coldly in my chest, chilling me with the truth. "No one has powers like mine. I can't die. No matter what they did, no matter how hard they tried, I always lived."

He lifted his head in understanding. "You were their first failure."

"I am their only failure."

I stepped past him to look out over the open cornfield. Brown and full of weeds, completely unused, forgotten. Each dead bush, each overgrown vine—all further proof that this was not the estate. That I was still free.

"Thank you," he said softly, "for helping us the way you are."

"It's just information. You guys already know a lot. I'm just filling in the holes." At least that's what I'd been telling myself.

"You're helping. It won't be easy talking about your family, but knowing what we are up against will be invaluable when the time comes to bring down one of your relatives."

I stared into the field, watching as the fog slowly lifted. "I could still run away," I murmured, not sure why I'd said the words out loud. Thirteen stiffened.

"Is that still an option you're considering?"

I jerked another shrug.

"Then you're not really free."

I turned on him with a glare. "Of course I'm free. I escaped, didn't I? I can make my own choices and go wherever I want."

"Of course you can make your own choices. But escaping was just the first step. There is still so much fear inside of you. It's not enough to be away from your father and uncles. As long as fear rules your decisions, you will never be truly free of your family." He put his hands on my shoulders. "Working with this team will be another step in helping you rid yourself of that fear. You need this, Magnolia, just as much as we need you."

I turned away from him.

A vision of Theo popped in my head. Held down in a field like this, his body drenched in sweat and blood. My father standing over him, killing him with unseen knives as Theo begged for mercy. Around them, the field was littered with the bodies of the rest of the team. My chest tightened in a painful ache. Pain pierced my side as if I were the one being stabbed. I stumbled forward. *No!*

The image vanished as quickly as it had appeared. *What the hell?* Thirteen steadied me. "What is it? What's wrong?"

"Nothing. It's nothing. I just—I was just thinking about what you said. What it might be like for your team if they tried to take down one of my relatives now. You know, without knowing what they were really up against." I looked back at the field. Still barren, but sunlight peeked through the clouds now, brightening the gray. "It was nothing."

Nothing except my option of leaving evaporating with the fog.

He watched me closely for a moment then said, "Come on," and indicated the direction of the farmhouse. "I'll walk you back." I stepped up beside him and together we made our way back through the woods.

What I felt for Thirteen was strong, but he had earned my trust and concern by keeping my presence secret all these months. He'd helped me acclimate to my freedom, taught me the basics of daily life like grocery shopping and debit cards. Theo had done nothing but sit there. And yet, the need to know everything about him was almost overwhelming. I wanted to touch him, to get in his mind and know what aggravated him or made him laugh. What was important to him. What he hated. What he loved. Had Theo done something to me? He must have a power I'd never heard of before or something. The way I felt when I looked at him, the utter terror I'd experienced at the mere thought of him being tortured by my family…

We stepped into the clearing just before the farmhouse and I realized I was hugging myself. I dropped my arms to my sides.

Screw this. Whatever he'd done to make me care so much, I was stronger. I had control over my feelings just as much as I had control over my powers. And I'd be damned if I let what I felt for him distract me again.

CHAPTER 7

It was still early in the evening when the sliding, crunching sound of cars on gravel came from outside. One of the hidden security monitors in the bedroom beeped twice. I grabbed my whiskey and waited in the kitchen.

Wonder if they will bother knocking, or just come right in?

A single beep sounded when footsteps hit the front porch. Everything was quiet for a minute, then they knocked.

"It's open."

They entered the kitchen in a single-file line. It was everyone from the meeting, minus Chang. Each one of them stared me down as they silently flowed into the cramped kitchen. Those who sat down did so in exactly the same order they had in the Thirsty Turtle's conference room.

Their faces were practiced blanks, every one of them completely devoid of expression. *Good.* They were tough, not dwelling on the trauma of my memory. They might actually be able to handle what I was going to tell them.

"Where is Thirteen?" Shane asked. He sat in one of the seats across from me, his thick arms crossed over his chest, his long blond hair hanging in his eyes. When I turned to him, his expression wavered, a flash of anger peeking through. He was seriously pissed off at me but his thoughts weren't giving specifics as to why.

"He and Banks are picking up some food," I answered. "They'll be here any minute."

And thank God for that.

Not that the room's awkwardness bothered me, but there was absolutely no food in the house. And I was starving. In fact, besides toilet paper, there were hardly any of the essentials. I'd brought my own whiskey, but with only two bottles left, even that was in short supply.

That reminded me. "Does, um, anyone want a drink?"

As soon as I spoke, I winced. What the hell could I offer them? Whiskey or water? And were there even enough glasses for everybody? *Shit.* My cheeks started to burn. *I must look ridiculous.*

"We're fine," Jon said. Then he forced a "Thank you."

I shrugged and took another drink. It was a strange silence, what with all of them staring at me, trying to be intimidating. I glanced across the table to Charles. He'd spent most of the day at the ER getting pins put in his broken hand. The cast was so huge his fingers weren't even exposed.

"We were hoping we weren't too early," said Cordele, fingering a lock of her hair. She needed to touch up her roots. Probably shouldn't point that out, though. "We tend to run ahead of schedule. The Network is kind of unnaturally efficient that way." Her eyes widened into perfect circles. She blushed deeply and looked at the table, hoping no one had actually heard her.

"No problem," I said. "I tend to be *unnaturally* efficient myself."

"We already knew."

Everyone's expression so perfectly mirrored one another's that it took me a second to pinpoint Charles's wife as the speaker.

"Excuse me?"

Marie's dark eyes narrowed. "We already knew that your family had powers. And that they've used those *abilities*—" she spat the word in disgust "—to torture anyone they wanted. Hell, the number of unexplained deaths in the pharmaceutical division of Kelch Incorporated alone should have them on the FBI's most wanted list. The whole corporation is just screaming 'front operation.' But they aren't even a blip on the feds' radar. Gun running, election fraud, illegal drug development, murder—no one can get away with that much illegal activity without leaving any evidence. Not without supernatural help. It's why the Network was created. Why this team was brought together in the first place." *So don't think you showed us anything special*, the last words heavily implied.

Her short hair had been styled into tight curls, emphasizing the pinch of her face. She squeezed Charles's good hand as she sat taller in her seat.

Well, wasn't she just the important little bitch.

I peeked into her thoughts. Ah yes, textbook alpha female. I was prettier than she was. Stronger, more powerful, and I had Thirteen's ear—all justifiable reasons for her to hate me before she even met me. How petty.

I moved my glass in circles on the table. "I'm well aware of why Thirteen brought this team together," I said evenly. "Apparently, you think you actually know something about who my family is and what we can do. In case yesterday's demonstration didn't clue you in—you know, the one where I used a power you didn't even know existed to push a memory into your minds—I'm here to show you just how much to have to learn. And, by the way, Thirteen already provided me with all your Network's evidence against my family."

"Does Thirteen know that he provided you all this evidence?" Theo asked. He leaned against the wall that separated the great room from the kitchen. I'd avoided looking in his direction but, damn, he just smelled so good. I braced myself and met his gaze. His expression was a familiar blank. But something inside me recognized him, and not just from yesterday's meeting. This was something more. Had I felt this yesterday? I didn't think so.

"Er, no. Not all of it."

The corners of his mouth wavered, struggling not to smile.

Heather leaned forward in her seat. "It was real, wasn't it?" she asked urgently. She'd given up trying to keep her expression blank. "What we felt and saw at the Turtle, in that tank with…" she shuddered. "That was a real memory of yours? That really happened to you?"

I took a long drink. My own face fell into a practiced mask.

"Yes," I said. "That happened to me."

Heather swallowed. "And other things? It was more than just that one time?"

"Yes. It was more than that one time."

"How often?" This from Shane. His blank face wavered when I turned to him.

"Every day."

Marie's tight manicure clicked on the table. She snorted. "I don't believe you." Images of me flashed in her mind. Pictures she'd studied from my family's Network file. A Senate campaign event, a Kelch Inc. holiday function—prestigious occasions held on the estate where I'd been dressed up and put on display. If only they had a photo of what had taken place after the guests said their good-byes.

She continued with her jaw set. "Obviously you can get inside our heads, but you probably just made up that whole scene so we would feel sorry for you or accept you without question. It doesn't work that way, little girl."

Little girl. That was cute.

My power rose like an electric current under my skin. I put my drink down so I wouldn't spill it by accident. Then my mouth twisted into an unpleasant smile. "What *you* believe really doesn't matter, though. Does it, Marie?" Then I took another drink and peered at her over the rim of my glass. Her face darkened in rage. To be so easily dismissed, she actually started to tremble. I smiled wider.

You're not the only bitch in the room, sweetheart.

Jon gently waved to Marie in a "settle down" gesture. "Let's assume for a moment that what we experienced yesterday was a real memory," he said. She ground her teeth but sat back in a pout. "What exactly did we witness? The water changed, but what happened to it? And how did you survive?" He raked me with his gaze while he spoke. He wouldn't find anything. I healed too completely to leave scars.

"You know," Charles said, leaning around Marie, "if what she showed us *was* real, that could explain Kazan."

"Oh my God," Cordele gasped, "he's right. All those men, with those burns all over their bodies. We couldn't find a cause."

Charles continued, "What was it, two days later that the Kazan State Technical University announced its exclusive agreement to collaborate with Kelch Incorporated on their aircraft technology?"

"Was there a sprinkler system," Shane asked, "in the warehouse where the bodies were found?"

Jon's calculating eyes remained fixed on me. "Yeah, there was a sprinkler system. No one thought to see if it'd been triggered, though."

"We need to go back and check that." Shane pulled out a note-pad and started scribbling.

Everyone turned to me. *Where the hell was Thirteen?* Jon saw my hesitation and frowned.

"If you don't mind," I said, as politely as possible, "I'd like to wait for Thirteen to return before we get into all the details."

That appeased Jon for the moment, but questions still bubbled in everyone's thoughts.

"Who was the third man?" Theo asked before the others had a chance. His dark hair fell forward to frame his face.

"I—I'm not sure who you mean," I stammered. *Shit!* I seriously needed to pull it together.

"In your memory," he explained. "Who was the third man?"

"Well, there was my father, Magnus—the one with the remote, and my oldest brother, Malcolm, then my other brother, Markus, and my two uncles, Maxwell and Mallroy."

Something sparked in Theo's eye and he turned to Jon. "So that's Mallroy, then."

The back monitor beeped twice. In the distance, an SUV approached.

"What happened to us—er—to you," Heather said quickly, "your legs…they were so…small. How…how old were you?"

The monitor gave a single beep as Banks's pounding footsteps vibrated from the porch. Heather's face strained. She didn't want Thirteen to see her reaction if my answer was as horrible as she believed it would be.

I leveled my gaze to look her in the eye. "I was nine."

The front door opened just as Heather raced past me to the small bathroom down the hall. As Thirteen and Banks entered the kitchen, the sound of Heather's heaves broke through the stunned silence.

CHAPTER 8

Apparently Chang wouldn't be a regular part of the team anymore. Oh, he'd do research and consultation crap, but Thirteen had approved his request for a "less visible role."

It wasn't like I gave a shit what any of them thought of me. Still, I couldn't deny the ache at knowing that one of them had officially requested *not* to work with me. I glanced at Theo. Then again, maybe that ache was from something else.

"So what exactly are we talking about here?" Shane asked Thirteen. "What kind of powers are we looking at?"

Thirteen turned to me. This was it—what I had agreed to from the beginning. I gulped down my whiskey and swallowed the nagging twinge of memories that threatened to resurface. With a deep inhale, I began.

"Well, while we each have the same base-level powers, our individual abilities vary. We all have the enhanced strength and speed that most supernaturals have. We each possess a level of telepathy that allows us to speak to one another mind-to-mind. Uncle Max has the ability of aggressive telepathy, or mind manipulation, and can also perform a mindsweep. Father has telekinesis. Very powerful telekinesis. Malcolm and Markus have both abilities, but to a much lesser degree."

"Why do your brothers have both telepathy and telekinesis when Senator Kelch and Magnus only have one or the other?" Jon asked.

"What Malcolm and Markus can do is nothing compared to Father and Uncle Max. Yeah, they can get in your head a little, or turn on the lights without touching the switch—but Uncle Max can erase your perception of reality, leave you a vegetable. Father can tear your limbs from your body without ever touching you."

My responses were practiced, my tone removed. I'd done everything possible to distance myself from the information I was providing. No reason to make this more personal than necessary.

Unfortunately, some things were just too close. There was no distance great enough to really remove myself from the brutality behind my family's power.

"She's getting stronger."

Father's voice echoed among the rafters. My heart sank to my feet. They hadn't used this old barn in weeks—not since their last round of experiments had gone so terribly wrong. I hadn't meant to shake the building's foundations or take off that guard's head when I reversed the motion on the chain saw. But I hadn't stopped myself when the power flew out of me either. He was right. I was getting stronger.

Footsteps beat across the cement floor. I huddled deeper into the dark corner of the loft. If only I could turn invisible.

"Mmm, she is healing faster than before," Uncle Max agreed. His loafers brushed the straw along the floor. I closed my eyes and made sure my mental blocks were cement against his intrusions.

"She'll be hitting puberty soon. I can't wait to see what becomes of her then." His sarcasm was thick and ignited father's anger like a match on benzene.

"I've tried everything!" Father shouted. "There is absolutely no reason for her to regenerate as she does. Majid found nothing obscure in her blood, and her DNA makeup is nearly identical to the boys."

"Your Doctor Majid is a biochemist," Uncle Max responded coolly. "His advances in chemical warfare may prove valuable when the time comes to negotiate that new plant in South America, but the pleb wouldn't know a DNA obscurity if it sliced open his nostrils. Not a bad idea, actually, but not the point right now."

We could always eat her. That way if she grew back, then it would be inside of us. I could use another set of arms to help with the horses.

Uncle Mallroy's thoughts slipped through the minds of his brothers. I held back a shiver. Mallroy's telepathy always came with a terrifying price: a glimpse inside the gray void that was his mind. And no matter how strong my mental blocks, that icy madness still brushed its way along my thoughts.

We tried to transfuse her blood into our systems when she was younger and it failed. Father's impatience clipped his silent words. It would be wasted time to try anything similar.

Uncle Max sighed, his feet still shuffling over the cement. "Your continued attempts on the girl's life tire me."

My chest burned from lack of oxygen, but I refused to risk the whisper that a breath might make. I could mask my power from them a while longer, but their senses were too strong. I needed to concentrate. Something had happened.

Uncle Max's voice was low. "What was the one contingency to your procreation, brother? The one absolute requirement behind

Mother's allowing you to bring that whore into our home and breed our line?"

A fissure rent the air. Power brushed against my skin. I focused all my might on my concrete mental walls.

"Control," Uncle Max hissed. "And you cannot control your creation."

The power turned hot, and I slammed my eyes shut tight.

"Don't you dare fucking mindsweep me, you son of a bitch!" Father's voice boomed. Uncle Max's power sizzled, and for a moment I couldn't tell who would win out—Father's telekinesis and physical strength or Uncle Max's telepathic rape.

The low growl reverberated against the walls of the barn. "I can control her," Father snarled. "Even now the child hides in fear of me! She may be powerful, but I am more. She is neither seen nor heard by anyone unless I…"

A slam. The cracking sound of bone on cement. Then terrible monstrous gnashing. I gasped, then quickly covered my mouth, halting the breath in my throat once more.

"But someone did *see her!" Uncle Max thundered.*

And not just anyone, *Mallroy added smugly.* Maxie's little press secretary, in all his painful colognes and sprays. Oh, he got a nice look at our precious Magnolia, didn't he? Wants her in the family pictures now. Won't that be fun?

"Then kill the bastard!" Father bellowed. "Erase his thoughts!" Then the tearing sound of flesh told me his mouth was otherwise occupied.

"I will not!" Uncle Max growled in response. "His West Coast connections are too valuable right now, and his mind is worn from all the alterations I've already made. Much more and the man will be totally brain-dead. Besides, I shouldn't have to do cleanup on this. It was your responsibility to control the child before she risked any further exposure."

"She will be controlled!" Father roared.

For a moment, something flickered among the three of them. Fear? It was gone too quickly to really sense. And I was too numb now to care.

I had been spotted by an outsider. There had been a slip in their tight control. No one was supposed to know about me. Ever. That way when Father finally succeeded and I stayed dead, there wouldn't be a need for explanations. But now…they wanted me in Uncle Max's family pictures? I could already feel the punishments after I smiled the wrong way or did the wrong thing.

However horrible my life had been up until this moment, I knew without a doubt that it was all about to get much, much worse.

"And Mallroy?" Jon asked, pulling me back to the here and now. "You mentioned the telepathy you share with each other, and strength you all have, and the, er, mindclean that Senator Kelch can do…"

"Mindsweep," I corrected as I took another drink. "Malcolm coined the term. Basically, he uses his telepathy to rip inside your head and scrape away whatever he wants, in the most painful way possible."

Jon's eyes narrowed. "Mindsweep, then. What special, um, abilities does your other uncle have?"

"Mallroy has the strength and speed, but his real power is in the way he can alter his appearance. He can do subtle things like change his eye color, or widen his nose, make himself taller or fatter at will. It's totally creepy to watch, but…that's Mallroy. Creepy comes with the package."

I took another drink. Against my will, I envisioned the clouded, swirling madness that lived in my uncle's mind. Nothingness, emptiness, a complete loss of humanity or control—it was the most terrifying thing I had ever experienced. More than any threat of my father's, that was for sure. A shiver crept up my spine as I pushed the image away.

"Mallroy doesn't leave the estate," I explained slowly, not meeting anyone's eyes. "He is…not like other people. Not even like the rest of my family. If we were normal, he would probably be considered retarded or deformed or something. But as it is, he is simply…maintained."

"What do you mean, 'maintained'?" asked Jon.

I hesitated, rotating my drink between my fingers. Major family secrets were on the horizon of this conversation.

"I'm not sure how to explain."

I spun the glass faster.

"It's like, to be able to do the things we do, there had to be something *more* to us. Something…other." The glass whipped around, a blur now, the whiskey rising up perilously. "That otherness is what gives us certain powers, and it's rooted in something very much *not human*. In Mallroy's case, the 'otherness' is more dominant than anything else."

The liquid spiraled, a cyclone hovering in the center of my glass. I let it spin for a moment longer, then abruptly stopped it. The whiskey fell, splashing around my hand. I licked my fingers and took another drink.

They all stared, faces slack, minds reeling with fear and amazement.

Thirteen broke the pregnant pause. "The source of the Kelch's abilities appears to be a paternal relative, but what caused the powers to develop in the first place is unknown. Understanding the strength and nature of what Magnolia has described, we have to assume that we are dealing with something other than the simple genetic anomalies we've come up against in the past."

Theo cleared his throat and leaned in. "What about you, Mag?" he asked. The tremor of his voice had my abdomen sinking. I scooted toward him automatically. *Mag.* My new favorite nickname.

"What about me?" I whispered. *God, was that really my voice?*

"What all can *you* do?" he said, then quickly sat back in his chair.

Focus, damn it! I had better control than this.

"Er, I don't know. I mean, the same stuff as the rest of them, I guess. I learned how to make myself invisible—a sort of survival mechanism, I guess. And I can heal myself. Obviously." Then I chuckled darkly. "I mean, how else could I have survived my life up until now?"

Cordele leaned forward, drawing my attention. "You. Can. Heal. Yourself."

"Yeah," I said. "I can regenerate the cellular elements of my body. My skin, my muscles, my bones, I can heal them as quickly as someone else can destroy them."

"So that's your unique power, then," Jon said, "healing yourself." He spoke more to himself than me so I just spun my glass some more and let my silence answer his question. I threw back the last of my whiskey and rose automatically to get another. I glanced around the table. *Screw it.* They knew everything now anyway. I reached out my hand and the whiskey bottle rose from its position across the room. It floated gently to the table landing directly in front of me.

Marie gasped. I bit back a smile. With my innocent face, I asked, "Anyone want a drink?"

I expected the silence to last longer.

"Sure," Theo said, a gleam in his eyes. "I need a glass, though, so if you want to just float one on over to me, that would be great." He leaned back in his seat, one ankle crossed over his knee. The pose more than emphasized his toned chest through his tight T-shirt. He took a deep breath and rolled his shoulders, stretching the shirt even tighter. He knew I was watching. Before I could stop it, my tongue ran along the edge of my bottom lip. Then I lifted my hand to summon another glass. Thirteen stopped me.

"Allow me," he said. There was an edge to his voice. I turned to face him. His eyes were hard and his mental blocks tight. *What was his problem?* He reached the cabinet and grabbed as many juice glasses as his fingers would hold. He slid one to Theo and then to several others who suddenly needed a drink as well. I passed around the whiskey.

"I think we've had enough demonstrations," he said under his breath.

CHAPTER 9

Six years old, I ventured down to the small third-floor kitchen to get something to eat. I wouldn't be invited to dine with my family until years later, and even then it was only when guests were around. But that night I'd healed several concussions and was feeling woozy. Maybe some bread would settle my tummy.

I'd just found a couple of croissants when I heard Uncle Max approaching. In a blur, I shoved the bread in my mouth and crouched in the shadows behind a plush bench. The space between the bench and the wall was so narrow, I almost didn't fit. Uncle Max never looked for me when I hid, but if he was here, then Father might join him. And I really didn't want to go back to the barn tonight.

"...so you thought I would somehow sway my brother's decisions on the matter, is that it?" His calm voice slithered over me. I shivered.

"A nephew at an Ivy League school would be perfect," Malcolm said. Uncle Max's power was so strong I hadn't even sensed my brother. But now, I could sense Markus there too.

"Just think about it, uncle," Malcolm continued. "A college-bound nephew will give you a perfect family-matters appearance. And the contacts that could be established in a fraternity or…"

"Enough," Uncle Max said softly. The fear around my brothers spiked. "So nice that you've taken such an interest in my recent political rise." Uncle Max opened the refrigerator. "What about you, er, younger one?" Uncle Max said to Markus. He poured himself some juice. "Do you share your brother's desire to leave his family?"

"I, I…that's not what he meant," Markus stammered. "He—I mean we—we just thought…"

"You just thought you would leave your blood, take the power it bore in you, and establish your own right in the world. How ambitious of you." He sipped his juice. "However, that is not your purpose. You are here to cultivate our power. Surely your father explained that to you. After all, the more vessels carrying our bloodline, the more powerful we will become."

I didn't understand that at first, but after a moment it made sense. Uncle Max, Uncle Mallroy, and Father were all strongest when they were together. Father could move heavier things with his mind, Uncle Max could probe more acutely into someone else's thoughts—and they were all faster when they were together. Did it work that way when they were around us too? I'd never noticed it before, but then again, I'd never thought to pay attention.

"But Magnolia has more power than anyone," Markus said. I stopped breathing. "As long as she's here—" his words cut off in a gurgled gasp.

"Your sister," Uncle Max said with disgust, "has power that will only weaken as she matures. She is utterly useless to us. If not for *your father's desire to keep her for his experiments, she would have been dead a long time ago."*

He was lying. My powers grew practically every day and he knew it. And God knew they'd tried enough times to kill me. So why the lie? I thought about looking in his mind to find out, but I was too scared about what I might learn. Finally Markus started breathing again.

"Of course, Uncle," Malcolm said after a moment. "It was an errant thought. Nothing more. Thank you for your time."

I stayed behind the bench for over an hour after they left. I was never going to leave the estate. Never. They would try to kill me, use me for their experiments, and that would be it—my life. Six years old, and for the first time, I prayed for a miracle.

Please, God, just let me die.

CHAPTER 10

I sat at the kitchen table next to Thirteen. He'd brought groceries again, just like he'd said he would, so when the others arrived for the next Wednesday meeting there was something to snack on. Not that anyone actually ate.

Heather smiled in my direction then quickly averted her eyes. Again. She'd been doing that for the last hour, wanting to bring me into the conversation but not sure how.

Why the hell she even bothered was beyond me. It was obvious that everyone else just wanted me to go away. Forget reading their thoughts. Their tense postures, the way they looked at each other but just glanced over me—no one wanted anything more from me. Especially Theo.

After a week, I figured I'd steeled myself enough that his presence would have no effect on me. Boy, was I wrong. The minute he'd stepped out of the car, my body had heated up. Then the sight of him stalking through the front door, a frown darkening his face…it was like I had no control whatsoever. I had to force my attention to everyone else, then fight to keep it on the conversation.

He was going through the same thing, too. And he hated it as much as I did.

As for the others, they were eager about giving their status reports. Apparently research was exciting to them. Analyzing the information I'd given them, listing out which new agents had gone missing, trying to pinpoint a weakness in my father and uncles—yeah, good luck with that one. They didn't seem to have accomplished much, but they were still upbeat, ready to do more.

I wasn't even sure why I was still being included. I'd given my information, and sure, I answered any questions they had, but for the most part I just sat back and watched.

Then Thirteen had an idea.

My stomach hit the floor when I saw his plans: Me. Training his team. Teaching them how to fight against my powers.

My skin tightened as power swelled in my veins. The only reason I didn't lash out at him was because of the innocence that coated his thoughts: Why wouldn't I train his team? It was an obvious next step, right?

He had no idea the implications of what he would be asking.

He didn't speak his thoughts out loud, but he knew instantly what I had seen. I waited for him to brush the idea away, dismiss it as an errant thought. But he held on, waiting until the updates were over. Then he turned to me, resolution hard on his face.

"You know the purpose of this team," he said in a low voice. The others milled around the kitchen, arranging plans for the day. "I don't want to lose another team member. Not when we have the resources to avoid it."

A resource. That's all I was to him now. *God, I was such a fool.* I should just kill him now and be done with it. Reach out, snap his neck. Or even better, I could just fry his heart from where I sat and watch as he crumbled to the floor. *This* was the betrayal I had been waiting for. I would have preferred a knife to the throat.

"Magnolia…" He sounded like one of those parents whose child was about to pitch a fit.

"You bastard," I hissed. My fingers curled into themselves, my nails sharp and digging into my palms. The dishes on the table started to shake. Then the dishes in the cabinet. Soon everything not nailed down would be trembling as I held back my power.

Thirteen watched me, confused. Banks moved into a defensive position at his side.

"You've already demonstrated the power of your family," Thirteen said cautiously. "Training would simply be a matter of more demonstrations."

"Bullshit!" I shouted. "You don't want another demonstration! You want me to teach them how to kill someone with *my* powers. You want me to give them the tools to go after *me*!"

Thirteen's face drained of all color. "No, Magnolia, no!" He reached out his hand to me and I jumped from my seat. Banks moved quickly, blocking me from Thirteen.

"Was this your plan all along, Thirteen?" I spat at him, my body aching. "Gain my confidence, get me to train your people, then, when I'd given you everything you needed, have them turn on me? Well, sorry to spoil your agenda, but if my father couldn't kill me after twenty-two years of trying, your pissant team of nobodies sure as hell won't be able to!"

"Magnolia, no…" Thirteen stood in front of me, pain plain on his face. I had to get out of there. I turned to leave the kitchen, but Banks blocked my exit.

"Get the fuck out of my way!" I shouted at him. Without hesitation, he scrambled to the side. His mind struggled not to obey my command, but it was pointless. I was too pissed to be subtle.

I maneuvered my way through the slew of kitchen chairs and around the corner to the bathroom. No one else tried to stop me. I latched the bathroom door and hugged myself against the sink. It was like my chest had been ripped open. *God, why did this hurt so much?* I turned and gripped the sides of the small pedestal sink and stared at myself in the mirror. My eyes started to burn.

Do not cry. Don't you dare cry about this.

I pictured Thirteen's face, the genuine pain that my words had caused him. Damn it, why couldn't he just be the callous bastard I wanted him to be right now? Why did he have to have such good intentions? It had never been his plan for his team to turn on me; I knew that. It was just—he chose me. He'd kept me safe, kept me secret, taught me how to live in the real world. He was supposed to care more about what I wanted than what was best for his stupid Network.

I wiped my face and took several deep breaths.

I wouldn't do it. Decision made, end of discussion. We'd agreed on my giving information. That was it. I was free now. No more torture sessions, no more hiding in shadows. I would not risk that freedom by teaching these people how to hurt me. Because no matter how sincere Thirteen's intentions were, his team would turn on me. I knew it without a doubt.

A knock on the bathroom door startled me. Boy, someone sure had balls.

"What?"

There was no answer. *What the hell!* I yanked the bathroom door open and froze.

Theo stood inches away, towering over me with his hands braced on either side of the doorframe. His face was dark, his hair falling over his eyes. My heart stopped beating for a few seconds. My breath caught the moment his scent filled my lungs.

His thoughts were in chaos—and so loud I couldn't have blocked them if I tried. He was drawn to me. A compulsion. Just like the pull I felt for him. And just like I'd been so sure that he'd done something to cause this pull, he was certain I had done something to him. That strange, warm place inside of me trembled, then grew. Against my will, I calmed down. My breathing steadied, my heart rate slowed. My rage at Thirteen lightened to a manageable pissed off. There was no motive behind Theo's presence here. He just *had* to be where I was. And I just *had* to have him here.

"You're not going to help us, are you?"

I jumped. Heather appeared from the hallway, breaking through our silent moment. Theo didn't move. I had to duck down to see her from under his arm.

"I've already helped you," I said coldly.

Theo's breath turned ragged over me. Ducking had moved me closer to him, and suddenly I had to be closer still. It was like a magnetic pull, stronger than anything I had ever experienced. The force of it put my family's energies to shame.

And it scared the crap out of me.

I leaped back in a flash, putting my back against the bathroom wall. Unfortunately, the bathroom was so tiny I was still only a few feet from the door. Heather peered at me from under Theo's arm. Her empathetic impulses alerted her to something heavy and sensual in the air, but she didn't trust herself.

"You're right. You have helped us," she tentatively agreed, looking back and forth between Theo and me. "But we won't be able to really stop your family unless you show us how."

Theo turned his head and glared at Heather. He didn't say a word, but his thoughts snarled at her.

Holy shit…he wanted to defend me. Rough stubble shadowed his jawline as he ground his teeth. A slight crook in his nose warned of long-ago fights. It was a fabulously sexy profile.

"Magnolia?" Heather said.

Theo turned an arched brow to me. Oh, crap; he caught me staring. Heat flooded my face.

"What?" I snapped, my voice cracking.

Heather's eyes widened. "I said, why not? Given what they did to you. So much horrible stuff that you had to escape. Why not help us defeat them?"

Because you would use what I taught you to try to hurt me. The words were on the tip of my tongue when Heather's mind swept over me. She was nearly a decade older than me, had worked for the Network for years. Yet she was more naïve to the world than I had been an hour after my birth. I felt the weight of Theo's stare. For some reason I couldn't crush that naiveté. Not in front of Theo.

When I didn't answer, Heather shook her head and walked back toward the kitchen.

Theo's grip tightened on the doorframe. With Heather gone, the connection between us flared. I clung to the wall because I wanted to go to him. Wanted to touch him, taste him.

His eyes twitched. Amid our overwhelming urges, something occurred to him. "Will you train us, Mag?" he asked softly.

My stomach dipped at the sound of his voice. Before I could stop myself, I nodded. His gaze softened and he leaned toward me. The fluttering in my stomach stole my breath. I had to get away from him. Now. Or God knows what else I'd agree to.

I cleared my throat twice then said, "I, um, need a minute."

He frowned. He didn't want to leave. I could feel the effort it took to peel his fingers from the door. With a shake of his hair, he turned away. I waited until his footsteps were past the kitchen and out the front door. Then I shut the door and locked it tight.

And cursed myself repeatedly.

CHAPTER 11

Everyone arrived the next morning at sunup, ready to start training. All because I'd said yes to Theo. I'd stayed up half the night trying to talk myself out of the decision. But the moment I pictured his face I was helpless to resist.

Thirteen had suggested I begin with my mental powers: telepathy, telekinesis, mind manipulation. Well, screw that and screw him. I needed a fight. And if I was going to do this, I was going to do it *my* way.

Nothing like a little hand-to-hand combat to start your day off right.

Before we could start, though, there was one little thing I had to take care of. With a deep sigh, I called out to Charles. He turned in the doorway to the backyard. The others were already outside. "You can't train with your hand like that," I said.

He faced me full-on. He was tall enough to make the hallway look tighter than it was. His buzz cut almost touched the ceiling.

"Thanks to you I don't have a choice, do I?" he growled.

"What's going on?" Marie said from behind him. Several others had followed her back into the house. Fabulous. We'd have an audience.

"Little Kelch here says she isn't going to let me train because of my fucked-up hand."

OK, *so* not what I'd said. "Of course you can train," I continued slowly, "I'll just have to heal you first."

Silence and blank expressions.

"You can really heal him?" Jon asked. I nodded. He looked back at Charles and shrugged. "So let her fix it."

"Are you serious?" Marie squealed. "Maybe you've forgotten, but she's the one who shattered his hand in the first place!"

"Then she should be the one to fix it," Jon said, his voice resolute.

For a long minute they all just looked at each other. Finally, Charles stepped forward. Marie sucked in her breath. I stared at his cast.

"Well?" he said.

It was going to hurt. Badly. I'd only ever healed another person once before, but Uncle Max had screamed like a girl when he'd made me fix that gunshot wound in his chest. And then he'd punished me with the drugs that he and Father had stolen from the Chinese politicians who shot him. After a moment I shrugged. Screw it.

I pulled out the sharpest steak knife I could find. Charles jumped back and clutched his hand to his chest. "What the hell?" he yelled.

"I don't think so," added Marie. She stepped forward to block me from Charles. It was a sweet move, actually, even if she was a raging bitch.

"I have to get the cast off. You can cut it off yourself if you want, but I can't do anything with that huge thing on your hand."

Marie snatched the knife. I tensed. She glared at me then handed the knife to Jon. It took forever for him to remove the damn thing. They were being so careful. I poured another drink and had it half finished by the time Charles rested his hand palm-up on the table. The others stood at his back, watching. I reached across the table. Charles flinched before I even touched him. *Oh, come on.*

"You have to hold still," I said. He scowled at me but took a deep breath and braced himself. I gently rested one hand on his forearm then hovered my fingers over the worst of his breaks. He flinched. Before he could pull away again, I lowered my fingers and focused my power into his bones. He gasped and jerked as if electrocuted. Marie and the others closed in behind me. I didn't stop.

Through gritted teeth a strangled cry escaped him. "Stop it!" Marie shouted right at my ear. I slowly turned to face her. She took a step back.

Finally, it was done—the bones healed around the pins from his surgery. I released him and he sagged to his knees, cradling his hand to his chest. I stepped around the table and lifted my drink.

With a toast to the others I said, "You're welcome. Now let's start some training."

...

Charles's hand was perfect. And after a couple of days of watching me fight, the scowls faded to reluctant respect. Unfortunately, it didn't last.

Theo lunged for me, armed with a stiletto. He spun, then leaped forward again in a move we'd practiced at least a dozen times. He missed, but his hand grazed my waist under my tank top. The moment our skin touched, power exploded between us. An electric current erupted, launching Theo through the air. I stood shocked as he landed on his back several feet from where I stood.

The others jumped to action. Shane guarded Heather and Jon as they rushed to Theo's side. Marie and Cordele took up defensive posts with Charles between them, each one ready to kill for their fallen teammate.

"You see!" Marie shouted. "She's using training as an excuse to take us out!"

The three in front went for their guns. I hunched in a defensive position, ready for an attack.

A crash at the house had us all turning. Thirteen and Banks raced through the back door, their movements tight with purpose. Another Network member had been found dead.

Our standoff instantly fell to the back burner. Thirteen and Banks gave orders, and the team moved without question. Theo got to his feet, rolled his shoulders in a stretch, then followed in pace behind Jon and the others. He didn't look back at me once.

Thirteen briefly nodded to me, but Marie was the only one to look back. She paused at the back door to glare at me over her shoulder. Then she slammed the door shut, leaving me alone in the field. The sound of their cars shook the air until they disappeared in the distance. Then all was silent.

I stared at the cloud of gravel dust covering the driveway, my mind numb.

I'd lost control of my power. The energy released at Theo's touch—I couldn't have stopped it. Not even if I'd tried. My knees gave out and I hit the ground. *What the hell was happening to me?*

I closed my eyes. Bright colors flashed in my mind. Red and yellow—the colors had haunted my dreams all week. On the estate I'd never slept soundly enough to dream. But here, I dreamed every night. Maybe that was the problem—I was too well rested.

I held up my hands in front of me. Power rose beneath my fingers then ran down my arms and into my chest. My whole body swelled with energy. I felt the power pulse, felt the strength of my muscles and the heat of my senses. Whatever had happened before, I was in control now.

CHAPTER 12

"This is bullshit and you know it!" I yelled at Thirteen from the front porch. Since I happened to be outside when he arrived, he hadn't bothered getting out of his car. Nice.

"I've done everything you've asked, Thirteen. There's no reason I shouldn't come. You just don't want to give up what little control you *think* you have over me."

"I never said that."

"Yeah, well, you thought it." Actually he hadn't, but I didn't care. I was pissed.

The funny thing was I hadn't even thought of joining the others on a mission until he suggested I shouldn't go. Now, I was adamant. Why the hell shouldn't I go? It wasn't like they were storming the estate or anything. They found fingerprints on the latest recovered body that led them to one of Uncle Max's public guards. As if going after a Kelch bodyguard was a big deal. Thirteen just wanted to keep me the Network's dirty little secret.

His hands clutched at the steering wheel.

"OK, you want the truth?" He looked up at me and squinted into the early morning sun. "The team doesn't quite trust you yet, Magnolia. You have no real field experience. They have no way of being sure that you'd have their back in a real fight."

"Of course they don't trust me! They're smart people, most of them. They *shouldn't* trust me. God knows, I sure as hell don't trust any of them. But that doesn't mean I can't go, that I have to stay here all the—"

"It's dangerous. This man works for your family."

I waved that off. "I'll stay invisible. I'll be prepared. Aren't you taking him into custody, anyway? He wouldn't get the chance to tell anyone even if he did see me—which he wouldn't."

He shifted the car into gear. "I'll call you later this afternoon."

"But, but…"

The car window started sliding shut. *Son of a bitch!* The porch creaked with my tempered power. "At least tell me where you're going!"

The window paused, nearly shut. The address popped into his head a split second before he blocked his thoughts. He met my eyes through the glass. The window slid back down. He pressed his lips together, then finally said, "I thought you didn't want this. Didn't want to give this much to the team. Hell, two weeks ago you were ready to kill me for asking you to train them. Now you want to join them on a mission?"

"Don't you dare put this on me!" The cement porch steps crumbled around the edges. "You are the one who put me in the position! You used my affection for you to ask more than we ever agreed to. Now I'm asking for something and you refuse. It's bullshit!"

For some reason I didn't want him to know that it was for Theo that I had agreed to train them; not him. But I'd dwell on those feelings later.

Thoughtfulness tightened his face. "If you really want to help the team on missions, then you can. But not today. Just be patient a little longer," he said, an order this time. "You are serving a purpose here, more valuable to the Network than you realize." His eyes narrowed. "Be patient, Magnolia. Don't…" His lips tightened into a hard line. "Stay here. I'll call you later."

With that he rolled up his window and drove off.

I listened as the sound of his engine faded in the distance. Then I counted to twenty just to be sure. He was gone. I ran back inside and grabbed my keys.

...

Sunlight blinded me in the rearview mirror. My hands rested on the dash as I idled in front of a gated entrance to some large private neighborhood. Thirteen and the others were in there somewhere, staked out in another Network agent's house. I scanned the road for Thirteen's SUV or Shane's truck, but there was nothing.

I pulled forward another half mile then parked off the gravel shoulder where my car wouldn't be seen. I pocketed my key and took a deep breath. My power stretched out until I was completely invisible.

OK, here we go.

I ran across the road and into the trees that surrounded the neighborhood. There wasn't an actual wall, just tight, tall trees that worked well as a border. Once inside, I followed the main road into the neighborhood's depths. The homes were large and set back on wide yards of grass and woods. About a mile in, the road split into a three-way fork.

Thirteen had given up the address, but without my car's GPS, I was lost. So I listened.

Nature rustled around me, animals and insects. Farther out, I heard the strum of golf carts, lawn mowers growling, the buzz of a couple of dozen air conditioners kicking on.

How big was this neighborhood, anyway?

I listened further until finally I heard the low static of a voice whispering through an earpiece. *Aha.* I moved in the direction of the crackly whispers, but after a few steps my feet grew heavy.

Was I really ready for this? The targeted home belonged to one of Uncle Max's old bodyguards. Some guy named George Batalkis. The name didn't ring any bells for me, but that only meant he'd been a public guard and not an estate guard. Still, was I really ready to face someone that close to my past?

A landscaped median, dotted with gardenias, split the pavement. My pace slowed to a crawl. I'd once worn an entire dress decorated with those damn flowers. The stylist had practically glowed when I stepped into the ballroom. I'd posed for the pictures, nodded when appropriate. I'd never smiled—that had been just impossible—but I'd attended enough Senate functions to know how to play the role well enough. Unfortunately, something had changed that night. *I* had changed. Puberty had struck, and with the gardenia gown fitted so perfectly to my new figure, no guest had been coherent enough to hear what Uncle Max had to say. The stylist's face flashed in my mind. Shock and pain had brightened her eyes when Uncle Max had garroted her after the party. She had gotten off easy—a quick death for a dress that fit too well. I hadn't been so lucky. After all, it was *my* fault all the men invited went dumb when I entered the room.

"zzzz...no traces of forced entry..."

Was that Charles or Jon?

"...movement on the north side...hold your position."

I dashed into the woods of the next yard. Shane was the first I spotted, crouched low behind a landscaped mound of bushes.

He wore all black, his eyes hidden behind dark wraparound shades, his blond hair pulled back in a tight ponytail. His thoughts were sharp, on the moment. The goal was to capture only. Later they would question Batalkis, find out about the Network agents still missing. The black body armor made him look even more muscular than usual.

I positioned myself next to him. He would hate it if he knew I was this close. I'd glanced inside his mind during one of our training sessions—my face had been all over his thoughts. It killed him that I was living in a house that his family had once owned. His parents had vanished after refusing to sell their land for one of many Kelch Inc. expansions. He'd thought it poetic justice that he gave the three-hundred-plus acres to the Network. Then I'd shown up.

Whatever. He could keep his scowls.

The targeted home was five thousand square feet of white brick. The driveway wound its way through the trees before disappearing at the neighborhood's main road. Secluded, nice—maybe this guy had changed roles, taken on a more lucrative position for my family. Something like kidnapping Network members, perhaps?

"All clear on north." Theo's muffled voice came through Shane's earpiece. North. I was moving before I even realized it. Jon's voice over the wire stopped me.

"Clear on east. Move in."

Move in? Instantly I listened to the home's interior. Nothing. No movement, no heartbeats or breathing. No one was home. Only the normal house sounds came from inside. That and the steady, almost silent beep of an alarm on the lower level.

I went in for a closer look. A few feet from the three-car garage, I froze. The air changed. Nothing looked different or smelled different, but a warm mist now hung all around me. The hairs on my arms rose. It felt…familiar.

My family had been here. And they had used their power; I could feel it.

A chill started up my legs and spread throughout my body. I'd never realized that our power left a physical presence. But I could sure as hell feel it now. I stepped back. Trickles of warmth drew over my skin, not pulling, just caressing—like leftovers of power used. It almost tickled.

A quick buzz came from the far side of house. A door clicked. Someone had disabled the alarm and was entering through a side entrance. Cordele. She knew no one was home and was looking for evidence.

I took another step back. The lingering power brushed against me again and I shuddered. Beep. Beep. Beep. The alarm from the basement quickened. So quiet, I knew their equipment wouldn't pick it up. But didn't she just disable the alarm…?

Oh God.

I raced to the front of the house. The front entrance steps were uneven and I tripped on the last step. My hip slammed against a large potted shrub next to the door. Dirt and bush exploded all around me. *Fuck!* I'd have a nasty bruise for about three seconds. With both hands I gripped the door's handle and yanked the entire thing off its frame. Tossing the door aside, I ran into the foyer.

Cordele was right there. Gun gripped in both hands. The barrel pointed right at me.

I leaped to the side, but she didn't shoot. And her aim didn't follow me. She held her position, her hands steady. Her clear, brown eyes searched the open doorway. Her hair was pulled back tight like Shane's, hiding the blonde among her brunette roots. She'd just watched an invisible force blow away a solid oak front door, not six feet in front of her, and she hadn't even flinched. My respect for her doubled on the spot.

The beeping raced, louder now that I was inside. We were out of time. I pulled back my power and revealed myself. My hands shot up as she turned her gun on me.

"Cordele," I said quickly. "Cordele, it's me. It's Magnolia. We have to get out of here. Now."

Her thoughts moved fast. Was this a Kelch trick? Had Thirteen sent me in? She hadn't been told of any change in the plan. So why was I here?

"Cordele!" I said again. Then I moved. In a blur, I twisted the gun from her grip and grabbed her from behind. Her gun arm wrenched awkwardly at her back, pinned in place against my chest. I picked her up in a bear-hug heave and lifted her feet off the ground. She struggled, but it was pointless. Then I ran.

I raced down the front steps and into the yard. Charles and Shane appeared from the tree line, guns up when they saw me carrying Cordele.

"Run!" I shouted. "There's a bomb!"

They paused, confused. I continued across the yard and yelled back over my shoulder, "Run, damn it, the place is going to blow!"

Shane kept his gun on me, but Charles put a finger to his earpiece and sprinted after us. A moment later, Shane followed.

I saw the main road up ahead when the deafening blast shattered the air around us. My feet flew out from under me. Cordele slipped from my grip and I let her go just as I slammed face-first into a gardenia bush. *Fucking flowers!* My legs collided with something hard and I hoped it wasn't Cordele's face. The wind whooshed out of my lungs on impact, but a second after landing, I was back on my feet.

Debris fell in chunks from the sky—pieces of brick, wood, plaster—all coated in a dense cloud of smoke. Cordele moaned from a few feet away. I walked over to her as she rolled onto her back, coughing.

"Are you OK? Cordele?"

Footsteps came from behind. I wheeled around, blocking Cordele. It was Charles. Gray ash covered him from head to toe. Shane appeared a few feet behind. I held my position.

"What the hell did you do?" Charles shouted at me.

"I just saved your ass," I shouted back. "You're welcome."

Shane checked Cordele for injuries.

"Fuck that," Charles said with a snarl, "you just about blew us all up!"

"There was a bomb, you idiot!"

"Bullshit! Our scanners didn't pick up anything. The only thing out of place in there was you." He raised his gun and aimed for my head. Instantly it turned hot in his hands. So hot the metal melted in his grip. *Holy shit!* I'd never done that before.

He cried out and dropped the weapon. His face turned red with rage. "Will you stop fucking up my hands!"

"Stop attacking me and I'll think about it!"

Tires squealed on the road ahead of us. A car stopped at the top of the driveway. Neighbors.

"Let's get out of here," Shane said, echoing my thoughts. "The others pulled back. We need to reconvene with Thirteen and Banks."

Charles didn't move. He had another gun at his waist. One with a rubber grip. Could he get to it in time? Before I tried something else?

"Now!" Shane ordered, then followed Cordele into the trees.

I waved for Charles to go first. He scowled. The neighbors' voices drew close. Finally he growled in frustration, then stepped back. I followed his lead.

I kept Charles in view as we made our way through the thinning smoke. A knot formed in my gut as we walked. So much for sneaking in on the mission unnoticed. Even worse, Cordele hadn't gotten the evidence she needed. The Network's most promising lead had just had his house blown to bits. I knew none of this was really my fault, but still.

Thirteen was going to kill me.

CHAPTER 13

I should have known today would be a total clusterfuck. Even before Thirteen told me training was canceled, even before I'd snuck out to join the team's mission—I'd woken up with a throbbing headache. Almost as bad as the ones I used to get while healing from Father's punishments.

It was the dreams. Abstract, swirling masses of dark red, every now and then a flash of yellow. Just thinking about it made me dizzy.

A chilly feeling trickled down my spine. Twice now my powers had acted in a way I hadn't expected them to. Theo being shot across the yard during training—I'd figured that was from whatever was happening between us. But melting that gun in Charles's hand…it was something I'd seen Father do before with his telekinesis, but I'd never done anything like it. Were these dreams more than just dreams? Was something inside me changing?

Sirens approached Batalkis's house. Several acres separated one neighbor from the next—probably enough to protect those living close by from the fires of the explosion. Not that I cared what happened to the neighbors, but still…

I stayed with Charles until we came to another brick house farther back in the neighborhood. It was a lot like the one we'd just left—large, secluded, well maintained. We walked around a pondlike pool and entered the home's lower level. The room was a game room—pool table, big couches, big-screen TV. The only other exit was the stairs. Right where Banks and Thirteen stood together, talking in low voices.

Banks looked up when we entered. Thirteen turned away. Great.

Charles met Shane at the pool table. Papers and surveillance photos covered the felt table in front of them. Their short-range scanners and monitoring equipment lined the wall behind them.

I took a seat in a recliner against the wall. Cordele stretched out on the couch across from me. She eyed me steadily, holding her rib cage. I rolled my eyes.

"Detective Pryor's on his way," Thirteen said into his cell phone. "He'll be your Network contact with the IPD. Stick with the neighbors until he arrives." Then he ended his call. I looked at my lap. The room stiffened as he walked over to stand in front of me. The corners of my eyes started to burn.

Don't you dare cry! Not in front of all these people…no matter how disappointed he is in you.

He crouched in front of me and waited until I looked up. This close, his huge body blocked the others from my sight.

"Are you OK?" he asked, his voice tight. I nodded. His big hand gripped both of mine in my lap. He took a deep breath. His mind was too focused to read, but if I didn't know better, I'd say he was holding back his own strong emotion.

"Did you blow up Batalkis's house?" he asked softly.

The burn in my eyes threatened real tears. I shook my head no and, fortunately, that was enough. Thirteen let out the breath he'd been holding. He nodded, squeezed my hand once more, and then joined the others to review the surveillance equipment readout.

...

Afternoon sun lit up the game room. I checked my watch: 3:08 p.m. *Shit.* This wasn't good. Thirteen stood over the pool table, Charles and Shane at his sides. Jon was on speakerphone. He and Theo were back at Batalkis's working with the police. Like Thirteen, they both had government credentials that got them past the yellow tape. I could ignore the burning twitch and the pounding headache if it was Theo calling in to report. But with Jon talking…I held back a growl. My hands moved over my arms. My legs crossed and uncrossed every few seconds.

"We've got a problem, Thirteen," Detective Pryor whispered through the cell phone. "Give me a second while I find a secure location."

That's it. I had to do something.

On hands and knees I scoured the entertainment center. DVDs, books, video games. *What the hell? Didn't these people drink?*

I tried to focus on just Cordele's thoughts, but it was no use; other thoughts kept slipping through. Shane was pissed—about the explosion, about missing Batalkis, about life in general. Then Charles—he was second-guessing his decisions, wondering how he could have prevented the house from going up in flames. And then there were even more: the fire crew at the explosion site, the neighbors who had come to watch. My head throbbed. I tore through another shelving unit. Jon's mind hit me. Then Detective Pryor's. I closed my eyes tight and held my fists to my temples.

"How long has it been?" Thirteen whispered from beside me. I jumped. I hadn't even heard him coming.

"This morning," I gritted out, "before you came to HQ."

"That was over nine hours ago. You didn't bring anything?"

I turned on him. "I hadn't exactly planned on being gone the entire freaking day!"

He grabbed my arm and yanked me to my feet. I twisted from his grip and fisted my hands. Lights flickered all around me. The TV shorted out.

It's Thirteen. Just Thirteen, not someone trying to hurt you.

But my mind was frazzled. I couldn't think. He stood his ground in front of me, once again blocking my view of the others. I met his eyes and suddenly saw an image of the farmhouse. The couches in the great room, the cobwebs in the kitchen. He was giving me something familiar to focus on. And it worked.

I followed the rise and fall of his chest. Breathe in, breathe out. All the while I walked with him through the mental layout of the farmhouse. The tacky kitchen. The tiny bathroom. My bedroom. After a moment, he motioned for me to follow him upstairs.

The stairs from the basement game room opened into a modern kitchen. Glass cabinets, stainless steel appliances, a tiled island centered in the room. Thirteen stopped and pulled out a bar stool. "Sit."

I glared at him but took the seat. He opened the cabinet above the stove and pulled out a brown bottle of Jim Beam. My arms trembled; the twitching went into overdrive.

"A couple of decades ago I was in Shanghai," he said. He opened a couple of other cabinets, looking for a glass. "The target was a fortune-teller. A swindler who bankrupted an entire village." He shrugged. "It was an entry-level assignment, but I was new to the Network so it was mine." He brought down two juice glasses and set them by the whiskey. My throat burned. "Turned out the woman wasn't clairvoyant, she was telepathic. She used the townspeople's thoughts to promise them their dreams, then emptied their bank accounts." He poured a couple of shots. My head pulsed.

"Once I had her in custody, she begged for her opium." He went to the fridge for ice. "We refused."

Was he going to withhold it? Drink it in front of me?

He plopped ice in both glasses then slid one of the drinks across the counter to me. "She killed herself within four hours. But not before tearing her own ears from her head trying to stop the voices." He met my gaze. "Her power was nothing compared to yours. I suspect the same is true for the pain."

I grabbed the glass with both hands and downed the drink. Instant coolness to the lingering burn. He slid me the second glass and poured another. The pain slowly faded. Another three glasses and I was alone again in my head.

"Thank you," I said finally.

He watched me with his back against the counter. "You want to tell me what happened at Batalkis's house?"

I looked at him closely. His thoughts were clearer now but I still didn't see a reprimand coming. I must be missing something. "Cordele and the others explained it enough," I said, circling the glass on the countertop.

"I'd like to hear your version."

I cocked a brow.

"An electric igniter was found among the rubble," he explained. "Our short-range equipment is stronger than our long-range, but it still didn't pick up the device when we did our initial scans. I know you didn't cause the explosion. But there are still questions. Jon said the police found human remains. We're trying to determine if Batalkis was home, setting off the explosion himself, or if the bomb was triggered from a remote and the remains are one of the missing Network agents. We didn't read any signs of life when we approached the house, so most likely the body was already there when the explosion occurred. Which leaves the question of how—"

"It was triggered when Cordele entered the house," I blurted.

He gave me a speculative look. I sighed.

"I followed right after you left," I told him. Then I explained everything. Crouching beside Shane, the bomb ticking, the door, Cordele—everything.

"There was something else, though," I said when I was done. "When I was in the yard I, um, felt something."

"What do you mean?"

"My family had been there. Maybe not today, but recently. I could feel it. It was like a shadow of their power was left behind. It was all around the house." I took another drink. "You know, I never thought about what it felt like to use our power before. It never dawned on me that there would be an aftereffect. But it makes sense, I guess. I mean, when you use the kind of power my family uses, there should be some kind of…impression or something, right?

He didn't answer, but he didn't have to. His thoughts were too concrete to hide. *Son of a bitch.* I closed my eyes.

"So that's it, then?" I asked, trying to contain my anger. "My punishment for not following your orders: you're going to make me fight. Put me on the front lines—see if my power can match my family's in a real one-on-one battle? Well you can go to hell, because I've already done my time, and I'm sure as hell not going back!"

"I will do everything in my power to keep you from coming face-to-face with your family," he said quickly. "You must know that by now. But you asked to join today. You fought me to be here then came alone after I refused." He took a deep breath. "I know I've already asked more of you than we ever agreed to. Today, when you saved Cordele, you proved that you're willing to do what's necessary to support and protect this team. If you want to just keep training, remain an invaluable resource away from the threat of action, I have no problem with that. But that's not what you wanted when you snuck out to come here today."

Actually going up against my father or Uncle Max—could I even do that? Like, physically, was it even possible? The thought of seeing any one of my relatives made bile rise in my throat. I needed more whiskey.

"I'll train them on some of the other powers," I said finally. "It's time to move on to something beyond combat anyway."

He nodded and I looked away. This conversation wasn't over. I knew that. But right now I didn't want to think anymore.

I threw back the rest of my drink. "When can I leave?"

He looked at his watch. "The team is meeting back at your farmhouse in an hour."

I rubbed my hands over my face. *Great.*

CHAPTER 14

A bagel in one hand and my whiskey in the other, I sat cross-legged on one of the ottomans in the great room. Theo sat across from me on one of the longer couches with Jon and Heather. Whatever it was that drew me to him, it was getting stronger.

Thirteen was all business. He'd been on the phone with Banks, and while nothing was official yet, the coroner on site thought the body found at Batalkis's house was Batalkis himself. We'd have to wait to find out how long his body had been there. Of course, if the corpse had been there too long, I would have smelled it rotting. No point sharing that, though. Didn't want to interrupt Thirteen when he was all-business mode.

Late afternoon sunlight streamed through the front window right into Thirteen's eyes. He kept moving around to avoid the glare. Curtains. How could I have gone this long without getting some?

"Chang is compiling a new list of all Kelch and Kelch Incorporated properties," Thirteen continued. "We will work on rotations—each scouting out a given site for likelihood of holding hostages. We will reconvene here in the morning to determine next steps."

Thirteen paused and took a shaky breath. There hadn't been any more bodies recovered, but at least three Network agents were still missing. Their absences affected him more than he wanted the others to know.

"Magnolia," he said. I sat straighter. "You said that your family's power was used at Batalkis's home. Something more than just their physical strength. Can you show us how to defend against what you felt?"

I nodded and shoved the last of my bagel in my mouth. I brushed away the crumbs from my shirt and quickly tried to piece together a good exercise to start with.

That's when I lost them. *Crap.*

All around the room, minds went numb. Hadn't they gotten used to me yet? I mean, seriously, a brush of my hands over my chest shouldn't send them all dumb and loopy anymore. I glanced at Heather and Cordele. Both women gave me arched looks. Then Marie. Her eyes were just as glassy and unfocused as the men's.

Well. That certainly added another level of hostility to the petty anger she continued to throw my way.

"Hey!" I yelled. "Snap out of it!"

Cordele swung back from her seat and whacked Shane on the side of the head. "Ow!"

"Well, it worked on Chang." She shrugged then flashed a smug grin. Everyone blinked themselves back to normal.

"You all know how fast I can move, how easy it is for me to incapacitate you. So when the time comes, remember, distance is best. If you *are* forced to fight hand-to-hand with one of them, remember the basics: they're all about speed and strength. Especially my brothers. Both have martial arts training but they didn't take it seriously. There's no thought in their fight—just quick brute force. And trust me, that can be enough."

I fidgeted with my drink.

"There's nothing you can really do about the telekinesis other than know that some of them have it. The main worry is their telepathy. Uncle Max is the superior power, obviously, but all of them can get in your mind to some degree. Only Uncle Max can rip out your thoughts in a mindsweep, but the others can mess with your senses, make you see things that aren't really there."

"What do you mean, make us see things?" asked Cordele.

"They can make things appear. Like they can put a wall in front of you, or make you think there are people yelling at you. It's all very real to the people who see it."

"Then how do we tell what's real and what's not?" Jon asked.

I looked at my glass and turned it in my hand again. "I'm not positive because they were never able to do it to me, but I think there's a way to block the illusion if you know it's coming."

"Is that something we can practice?" Theo asked.

"Sure," I said, an unfamiliar purr suddenly dropping my voice. "Wanna have a go?"

Shane's mouth went slack. Charles shifted in his seat. Theo fought back a grin.

Holy shit—did I just say that?

"Sure," Theo said. "Where do you want to do it? In here OK, or you looking for something more…comfortable?"

My face burned. Jon coughed loudly and shot Theo a look. I tightened the grip on my glass and took another drink. *Focus.* But God, it took all my effort not to get up and cross the room to him right now.

"There's always some sort of stirring when energy is used. It may be very subtle, but it's always there. Like at Batalkis's house. The power actually hung in the air and brushed against us."

"But only you could feel that," Charles said, impatience heavy in his voice.

"Yeah, but if you knew what it felt like then maybe you could feel it too." Everyone sat forward in their seats. Not a ringing endorsement, but I'd take it.

"I'm going to change something in the room," I said, very businesslike. "But I want you all to close your eyes so you can't see it."

Thirteen smiled to himself. "Excellent," he murmured.

"Close your eyes and let me know if you feel anything different."

When all their eyes shut—Marie being the last to comply, of course—I conjured a crystal chandelier onto the ceiling. A beautiful antique, it had gold leafing intertwined with crystals in three descending layers. It was just like the one that had hung in my nursery when I was a baby.

As soon as it appeared, Theo and Heather shifted in their seats.

"You can open your eyes," I said. Quiet gasps hissed through the room.

"Did anyone feel anything?" I asked.

Theo narrowed his eyes at me. Heather looked at the others.

"Heather?"

She jumped. "I, er, I don't know," she hesitated. "I don't think I felt anything, but I don't know."

"The moment I conjured the chandelier you shifted in your seat."

"Yeah, my legs started to fall asleep," she explained. "But that's not anything unusual. I've always had bad circulation, and my hands and feet fall asleep all the time."

I shot Thirteen a look and met his knowing gaze. Heather had more power than she realized.

I turned to Theo and this time welcomed the dip in my stomach. "Um, what about you? You also shifted as soon as I used my powers. Did you feel something similar?"

"No," he said after a long moment. "It wasn't like that. But I knew that you had done something."

"What did you feel?" Cordele asked eagerly.

Theo's frown turned dark. "Nothing. I felt nothing. I just… knew."

My heart stopped. *Oh my God.* Theo hadn't felt the movement of power in the air, he'd felt *me*. He recognized the power only because *I* was the one who wielded it. I rubbed my face with both hands. This connection with Theo was getting intense. Dangerous.

"OK," Jon said, dragging out the word, "but for the rest of us who didn't *just know*, how are we supposed to figure out these illusions?"

"How about you all just try to see past the illusion I created?" I said finally. "Since you know it isn't real, and you all certainly know your own minds better than I do, you can use your own defenses to push it out and see what's really there."

A few people nodded. Good enough.

"You know the chandelier isn't real. So see what's really there, then."

Everyone looked at the ceiling.

My breath caught when Theo turned to me. It'd only been a few seconds. He didn't say it out loud, but I knew. He had dissipated the illusion. Not because he had the ability to see past the power, but because *I* did. Our eyes held and the butterflies in my gut grew into a painful swarm.

Silently he mouthed the words, *We need to talk*. Something low heated up inside me as I watched his lips move. So warm, so soft against the dark stubble along his jaw. He seemed to almost glow as the heat inside me spread. I nodded.

Heather gasped. I took a shaky breath.

"H-how did you do it, Heather?" I asked.

"I don't know, really," she said, practically bouncing in her seat. "I just knew it wasn't really there so I thought about what *was* really there. Like the cracks in the ceiling that make out the shape of Bill Clinton's head, and the cobweb that's been hanging over the doorway to the kitchen forever." *Man, I really needed to clean this place.* "And once I focused only on what was real, the chandelier was just, gone."

"OK, good," I said. "Now everyone else try to do that."

They squinted hard at the ceiling this time. I made a point to focus on each one of them. "I did it! It's gone!" Cordele yelled after another minute.

"Me too!" Jon said then sat back in satisfaction.

Another two or three minutes later everyone had erased the chandelier.

...

"OK, let's try something different," I said, fanning myself. We'd been practicing for over an hour. The house had turned into an oven and the warm cross breeze from the open windows felt more like the night's sweaty breath than anything helpful.

I reached behind my ottoman to the floor next to me and conjured a stack of twelve-inch candles as if they had always been there. I handed the stack to Charles, who took one and passed the rest to Marie, who did the same until everyone had a candle.

"These are fast-burning candles," I explained. "They will be completely melted within a matter of minutes. Hold one tightly in both hands. You have approximately three minutes before the candles completely melt in your hands. I suggest you concentrate."

This was a good exercise. Motivating and innovative.

"It's going to *burn* us?" Charles asked.

"Not if you can recognize it isn't there," I retorted. Geez, if a little hot wax made them whine, what they hell were they doing going up against my family?

He growled low and shared a glance with Shane. Both men were especially frustrated. It made sense, of course. They were the executors of the group. Foot soldiers. Without a clear method to attain their goal, eliminating the illusions was a challenge.

Instantly, the candles were lit.

Theo and Heather vanished their candles immediately. Thirteen and Cordele in the first minute. I gave Thirteen a small smile. He didn't usually participate in training, but I should have known he would be at the top of the class.

No one cried out when the wax began to drip, but those still holding their candles strained against the burn. Charles inhaled on a hiss as the hot wax coated his fingers. Everyone else had dissipated the illusion. I waited for the wax to harden on his hands, then vanished the illusion. He flexed and turned his hands slowly.

"It's no big deal," Marie said softly. Charles pulled away from her.

"This is insane!" he yelled. "How are we supposed to fight against pain that real? That pain was real! Anyone who felt the wax burn their skin knew the pain was real! If this is what we're up against, it's impossible—it's suicide. They could throw fire at us, or run us over with a truck, and the pain would be real!"

"It's only real if you let your mind accept it as real," Thirteen said calmly.

"Yeah, well, when my hands are on fire, I'm sorry but that just seems real to me!"

"That's why we're practicing, Charles," Thirteen said, his voice rising. "Why we're so grateful to Magnolia for demonstrating, once again, the level of power we are up against."

"Grateful," Charles snorted. "Yeah, let me just give the girl a fucking hug for kicking my ass and frying my hands. Again!" He stood abruptly and ran a frustrated hand over his buzzed hair. "This whole thing is bullshit!" He plowed out the front door, slamming the screen in his wake.

Marie sighed. "Maybe we could take a break?"

Her concern for her husband raised my respect level to the point of actually having some. Charles, on the other hand, was pissing me off. Pain was part of the territory when it came to my family. Surely they all knew that by now. Even more, he had totally doubted himself after our little standoff back at Batalkis's. There wasn't room for second-guessing when it came to the Kelches. A lack of confidence would get you killed.

Chapter 15

The moment Thirteen agreed to a break, the cell phones came out. No one but Thirteen ever called me, so I fixed another drink.

I leaned against the sink, dropped some ice in my glass, when suddenly every molecule in my body started heating up. *Theo.* Glass in hand, he walked toward me. I averted my eyes and shifted out of his way. He stumbled. The glass in his hand slipped. We both moved to catch it. His arm brushed mine.

Instantly, a current of energy opened between us again. Sizzling, intense. Just like when we'd been training with that stiletto. Only this time, Theo was ready for it. He grabbed hold of my arms before he could be thrown back. The power reacted, shifted direction. Instead of throwing us apart, energy began holding us together. Like a thick cord, it wrapped around me. *Oh God.* I couldn't move away. Then I stopped trying. A vibrant image flashed in my mind.

His body, sculpted muscle rippling under soft masculine skin, pressed down on top of me. His weight heavy and warm. Flesh on flesh, his dark, gentle eyes boring into mine. Was this memory? Fantasy? I couldn't tell. And I didn't care.

Then came the feeling. Warm and wonderful—peace. The comfortable calm I'd felt that day in the bathroom transformed, became so much more. A powerful serenity settled into every part of me.

My mind pulled back. *NO! Impossible! Not real! Never real!*

With a flex of power, I leaped away in a blur. My heart pounded. My breath struggled in my throat. "What the hell are you doing?" I screamed.

"I didn't do anything!" he yelled back. He braced himself on the counter, panting.

"Bullshit!" I shouted again. "You're trying to get in my head!" But that was wrong. He didn't have supernatural powers. Something else forced that image and those feelings inside me. "Leave me alone!"

I ran to my bedroom, my legs trembling. I slammed the door. Locked it. Then barricaded myself against it. My arms clutched at my stomach. Theo's beautiful face, poised above me, tight with intent—it was all I saw when I closed my eyes. The comfort in that moment, the peace…it was agonizing.

I knew pain. I knew fear. Those feelings were constants and could be trusted. Moments of quiet or warmth—they only meant that punishment would be coming soon. I'd had months to adjust to Thirteen's kindness and I still didn't trust it all the way. Everything with Theo was so fast, so intense. There had to be something wrong with it.

Images flashed in my mind. Father's hateful mask. Mallroy's terrifying mind. My brothers—so handsome, so horrible. The red of my dreams, so much like blood it frightened me. The tranquility that wrapped around me at Theo's touch—I couldn't feel this way. It was too dangerous; it made my guard drop, shifted my focus. My knees buckled and I slid to the floor. I knew where my thoughts were headed, and I didn't want to go there.

But it was too late. Memories assaulted me.

...

Something covered my face. I sucked it into my mouth when I tried to inhale. Netting? A thin cloth of some kind? I went to remove it but my arms were bound tightly to my sides.

Insects burrowed into the earth around me. The smell of dirt and sweat and dried blood filled my lungs. Buried. I was in the ground, tied, and left for dead. Again.

I wrestled myself free from the binding and dug my way to the surface. Ten feet. I clawed through ten feet of packed dirt and mud and mulch before gasping the cold winter air.

Father's imagination was waning. He should have used chains.

For several seconds my eyes adjusted. I shivered in the cold. I had on nothing but cotton yoga pants and a sports bra, both shredded and crusted with dry blood. No wonder I was freezing. It took a few moments more before I recognized my tomb. Uncle Mallroy's ancient tool shed. I was on the far west acres of the estate. With a brief look around, I began the long trek back to the main property.

Keeping to the woods, I used the trees to block the icy winter winds. Dusk was near. When darkness fell the temperature would follow so I moved as quickly as I could. But my muscles were tight and sore. How long had I been down there?

I'd managed about twenty acres when I heard the deep, accented voices of two of the maintenance crew. I crept closer. They were loading debris into the back of a work truck.

"...days and nothing," the first one said. "I think they might have really done her in this time."

The second scanned the darkness while he spoke. "I heard the older son, the one with the eyes, bragging to the animal brother that he had bested her in some duel—took off her head."

"Yeah, right," the first scoffed. "None of them could take her and they know it. She probably escaped."

Escaped?

"No, no," the second argued, still looking over his shoulder, "the snotty one, he took the brothers to where they buried her. Said he and the other one sliced her head off. Brothers must've had proof because Celia heard them talking about using staff soon."

Both men shuddered, and then they hopped into their truck and drove away. My mind worked furiously, replaying their words and thoughts again and again.

My father thought I was dead?

I had been buried for days. Days. I looked down at my clothes again. I'd worn this the day Father had me in one of the old grain silos. He'd hung me upside down from chains before searing my stomach and back with a serrated horse whip and then burning me with a cattle prod. Gotta love farm life. But I'd freed myself from the chains and walked back to the far wing of the main house.

Or had I?

No, I'd never made it back to the house. I'd walked to the southern gardens when...what? I was shot. In the back. No voices, no movements, but a thought, a train of thoughts in the distance from the one with the gun.

Markus.

That little pissant had shot me! God, what a fucking coward!

I'd fallen, but not from the wound. The shot wasn't a bullet, it was a dart filled with one of Father's experimental drugs. In the next moment, Markus and Malcolm had sneered down at me, their handsome features twisted in grins of deluded pleasure.

I'd only registered the blade for a moment, recognized it as one of Father's favorites, and then the pain had hit me. Cutting, burning, I'd reached for my throat but I couldn't move past the drugs. I had tried to scream but no longer had a voice. They'd decapitated me.

An icy breeze cut through the trees and I shivered. With shaking fingers I touched the fresh sleekness of new flesh just beneath my chin.

I looked up to the dark and cold sky, blanketed in clouds waiting to snow. And there, forcing back the clouds, was the moon. Bright…and full.

The next thing I knew, I was moving. Running. Within seconds I was back inside Uncle Mallroy's shed.

I wrapped the sheet that had covered me in a tight ball before throwing it back into my deep hole. With my powers, I quickly packed in the upturned dirt and debris until it looked as if it had never been disturbed.

And then I ran.

Faster than the cold, I ran. And I didn't stop. Not for the wall surrounding the estate—doubt and hesitation had me pausing for only an instant—and not for the sounds of movement behind me. I ran until I was a good five miles or more from the estate, safe on the empty highway.

In a heap, I collapsed on the pavement. Release poured out of me in sobs. That's when the SUV struck me head-on.

I woke in the backseat of a moving car. The expensive leather interior and spot-on detail were of true luxury. I panicked. They weren't taking me back. I wouldn't let them.

Silently, I reached up behind the driver. In a blur, I wrapped the seat belt around his neck and pulled. The car swerved, knocked me off balance. The seat belt slipped from my grip. I fell to the floor as the car squealed to a stop. The driver scrambled out of his seat and wrenched open my side door. I attacked. A lifetime of being put down for even attempting to fight back had me clinging to this stranger and not letting go.

His head banged against the pavement as I pounced. He was enormous—my hands couldn't close around his thick throat. I ripped open his mind in a mindsweep, tearing into his most recent thoughts in the most painful way possible. His eyes closed tight and he shrieked in pain.

His mind held nothing of the estate or my father. But there was another face I recognized. Carter. One of Uncle Max's personal secretaries.

But this big man hadn't taken orders from Carter, he'd interrogated him. He'd held Carter for hours, launching question after question about a meeting Uncle Max had with some Egyptian diplomat. Then about the newest Kelch Inc. product launch. Then about my family's supernatural abilities. Who the hell was this guy?

Every time Carter had balked in responding, this man had hurt him. Badly. But Carter worked for my family. He knew what would happen if he talked. The man had turned his back for a second when Carter pulled a knife from the guy's back pocket and slit his own throat.

The guy had been horrified, but frustration had surpassed any other thought. He'd left Carter dead on a cement floor. Five minutes later, he had plowed into me.

I pulled out of his mind. He trembled beneath me. Slowly he opened his eyes. He looked familiar. Had he been to the estate? My hands still choked him, but he did nothing to fight me off. His eyes stared up into mine and I knew that he recognized me.

"Who are you?" I shouted.

He opened his mouth but only a gurgle escaped his bruised throat. I loosened my grip. "Thirteen," he muttered after a moment. I recognized the number as a name; one from my father's thoughts. No wonder he knew our secrets—this was an enemy.

But wait—was he my enemy?

I let him go and he fell back against the pavement. Now what? Steal his car? I couldn't drive. Run some more? I had nowhere to go. Warily, I eyed him. He was shocked to actually meet me. He hadn't been sure my brothers and I really existed outside of files. His thoughts were so honest, I didn't understand them. I kept waiting for a plot to use or hurt me. Or an intention to return me to the estate. But there was only curiosity and concern. And amazement.

I knew the evil inside him would come out eventually, but I would see it before it surfaced. So when he suggested driving me to one of his safe houses, I let him. He couldn't hurt me the way Father could. And after a few hours in a warm place, I could come up with a plan.

He never tried to hurt me. Not once. Instead he had offered me shelter, food, and the first kindness that I had ever experienced.

But when Theo touched me…it was so much more than kindness. It was peace. And that peace was so unbelievable that I knew it had to be just that: something not to believe in.

CHAPTER 16

I opened my eyes, my back still against the bedroom door, my legs still folded in front of me. Voices carried from the other rooms. How long had I been back here?

Slowly I stood and wiped a hand over my face. I tried to take in the room around me, but all I saw was the dirt of the shed floor, the pavement as Thirteen's car crushed me. The look in Theo's eyes.

"…nobody cares about that, Heather." Marie's shrill voice brought me back. "Whether she was *really* attacking Theo or not doesn't matter."

Nice. I'd had worse wake-ups, but still. Whispering about me from the next room over? Did they seriously think I couldn't hear them?

"Look, I know we all agreed to work with her and listen to her," Marie continued. "But I've been thinking about this lately. Network members didn't start disappearing until after she was already living at Thirteen's safe house. How would the Kelches know who was even in the Network? *We* don't even know who's in the Network, but suddenly the Kelch family has the inside track on how to capture any one of us? She's a plant, Thirteen. I'm sorry, but she is. And I for one am done getting all chummy with her and making her job that much easier."

The bulb in my bedside lamp shattered. It should have been Marie's head.

"I understand your concerns," Thirteen said, not whispering at all. "She's powerful. She's a Kelch. It makes sense that you would be wary." His voice got hard. "But the fact remains that she is a part of this team now. *My* team. She has trained you, provided crucial information to you. And this morning, she even saved some of you. If you still do not feel comfortable working along-side her, then by all means, let me know. There are plenty of other missions I can assign you."

I brushed the hair out of my eyes. After everything that had happened these last couple of weeks—my rage at being asked to train, disobeying his orders—he still took my side.

In her mind, Marie fumed. Being picked for Thirteen's team had been a privilege. Reassignment, even requested reassignment, would be a total slap in the face. And it would be all my fault.

No one spoke when I entered the kitchen. I went straight to the fridge and took down my whiskey. I didn't look at Thirteen, or Heather, or anyone. Not even Theo at the other end of the table. What had he said during their little "trust Magnolia" debate?

Marie leaned with her bony ass against the far counter. I poured my drink. Slowly I met her eyes. She gulped. It wasn't nearly satisfying enough. I wanted to see her shaking. Her face paled as her thoughts finally caught up with what the rest of the room had already figured out.

That's right, bitch—I hear everything.

Thirteen's cell phone rang. Several people jumped. Jon cursed under his breath. Thirteen looked at me as he answered, his face set in a dire warning.

Do not touch her, Magnolia.

Gee, was I that obvious?

I nodded to Thirteen's thoughts. He turned to finish his call in the great room. Marie's hand shook as she took a drink. Good. Almost immediately, Thirteen came back.

"Chang has finished getting the property details. We need to survey them immediately."

Chairs scraped the floor, hands grabbed at the food, bodies struggled to exit the tight kitchen. Even though she was farthest from the door, Marie was the first out of the room. *Yeah, you better run.* Thirteen stood across the table from me. The softness was back in his eyes—warm now with genuine concern.

"I'll call you soon," he said. I gave him a small smile. *Go get 'em, Thirteen.* I didn't say it, but for the first time, I meant it.

I shook my head and took a long swallow. God, now I was as delusional as the rest of them.

CHAPTER 17

The next couple of nights I hardly slept at all. When I dozed, my color dreams were especially vivid—tinted with that oh-so-fabulous unease and confusion that constantly rode shotgun in my life these days.

When dawn came after the third sleepless night, I grabbed my whiskey and an apple from the fridge and decided to take back my control: I was going to decorate. After all, curtain therapy was as good a distraction as any from my current emotional landslide.

I'd *finally* picked up some sun-yellow sheers the day before at a Super Target. The quality was horrible—nothing like the thick silk drapes used at the estate—but they were *mine*, so they were awesome. Shopping still sucked—all those strangers going loopy when they looked my way—but I was getting better at the whole normal thing. I'd even picked up some decent groceries while I was there.

I was hanging my new sheers in the front window when Thirteen's car pulled up the drive. He parked in the grass. Heather emerged from the passenger seat of his SUV. Maybe this was more than just the situational update I expected.

I opened the front door as they approached. Thirteen looked serious as ever, but Heather had a wide smile brightening her face.

"Nice curtains," she said as they came through the door. "When did you get those?"

"I did a little shopping at Target last night. With everyone out scouting buildings and businesses, I had some free time."

Her head tilted a little as she eyed me. The question was loud in her mind, but she thought it was rude to ask. She was right, but I answered anyway.

"I have my own money," I said deliberately. "An account with my mother's maiden name. It has money from her family that my father doesn't know about. So yeah, I paid for the curtains."

Her cheeks reddened. "I didn't think that you stole…"

"Yeah, you did."

Against my will, an image of my mother flashed in my mind. *Aged long past her years, eyes half crazed, she was still beautiful. I had her hair. And her lips. I hadn't seen her since I was a toddler, but that night she'd left her suite to ambush me in the eastern gardens. She took in my torn and bloody clothes, the quickly healing wounds, and spoke in a fast whisper. Her voice was scratchy, as if she hadn't spoken for years. There was an account, she said, created in my name, using her grandmother's maiden name. All her father's family inheritance had been funneled into it. The account was unknown to my father—she swore she never once thought of it—and supposedly untraceable. Then she disappeared into the shrubbery.*

Two days later, the newspapers announced her death.

A chill ran up my spine.

I walked Heather and Thirteen into the kitchen. "We found a building," he said, "a Kelch private holding that we didn't know existed until now. Chang found it among some sealed title work from the seventies. Another Network team scouted the building and they found something. Evidence that David Sasser had been held there."

"David Sasser?" I had to think for a moment. "One of the missing Network members. The guy you thought might have been at Batalkis's house."

Thirteen nodded.

"We want you to come with us!" Heather exclaimed. "To check out the place like you did at Batalkis's!" She glanced at Thirteen and stifled some of her enthusiasm. "Everybody else is still checking out other locations. I offered to accompany you and Thirteen to this new location."

I looked back at Thirteen. Obviously he wasn't as excited about this field trip as she was.

"Why do they think Sasser was there?" I asked.

Thirteen hesitated as Heather turned eager eyes to him. "There was blood," he said finally. "And, er, fingerprints."

He was holding something back. I peeked at his thoughts but his mental walls were rock solid.

"Well, let's get going," I said and threw back the rest of my whiskey. I slid on my shoes and followed Heather to the car. She took the backseat.

"You seem awfully excited about going to a crime scene," I said to her.

She tried to hide her lingering grin and failed. "I know, and it's just awful of me. I've never met David, and I'd probably be a lot different if we were going somewhere else, but I hardly ever get to go to the crime scenes. I do research for the Network more than anything else. But when I found out that he was going to have you come out and look at the site, I begged Thirteen to let me come this time."

She looked a little sheepish. *What do you know? I had a fan.*

About twenty minutes later we turned onto a worn side street just south of downtown. Three buildings were crowded next to what remained of a gas station. The long exposed wall of the end building was decorated with colorful gang graffiti, and all three storefronts displayed handmade "For Rent" signs. Thirteen parked in front of the last building.

The windows were barred and the front door was chained shut so we walked to the alley next to the building. Thirteen had a key. I didn't ask how—the man had access everywhere—and we let ourselves in.

The floor inside was littered with papers, trash, and leaves that had blown in from a broken window somewhere in the back. It was hot as a sauna and the heat only amplified the stench. Thirteen directed us down a hall, past empty offices on either side, until we reached an open area in the rear—a storage room most likely, given the shelving units on the far wall. In the center of the floor sat a plastic waiting room chair, spattered with stains of brown and red. Blood.

I took a step closer. Heather gasped and I stopped.

"Oh my God," she whispered, her voice trembling. "What *is* that?"

She pointed to the chair and at first I didn't see anything. But then I saw it, hanging from a string off the back of the chair. I inched forward to get a better look. Thirteen mirrored my movements, walking around the other side of the chair until we were both facing what appeared to be half of a hand—a thumb and two fingers—dangling from a long piece of stringy flesh off the back of the chair.

I looked up at Thirteen. "Fingerprints?"

He nodded.

"The blade must have caught on some of the flesh," I said, "peeling off this long string of skin in the process. Then it got stuck in the crack of the chair here at the top, and whoever was playing butcher was too busy or too cocky to care and just left."

Thirteen crouched down on his haunches to examine the fingers closer. I looked around the room for anything else that might have been left behind. Then I saw Heather. Her arms were wrapped tightly around her stomach, her face white and pasty as soap.

"Heather? You OK over there?"

She slowly shook her head back and forth.

"Heather?" I said again and turned to Thirteen.

He went to her and put a big arm around her shoulder. "Close your eyes if that helps," he said softly. She did, then buried her face in Thirteen's chest.

He looked back at me, his face still the same serious expression he had when he walked into the farmhouse. "What do you feel, Magnolia?"

Oh, yeah. I was supposed to be sensing the power here. Right.

I concentrated on the air in the room. The dank smell of mildew and sweat hung heavy in the room. Somewhere an animal had made a nest among the debris. The breeze from the broken window brought in scents of asphalt and garbage bins. But that was all.

"I don't feel anything here," I said finally. "Nothing. There's none of the lingering power that was at Batalkis's house."

I slowly moved around the room, frustrated. I must have missed something. That *was* David Sasser's hand hanging off that chair, and he *had* been taken by my family. So there had to be power in the air somewhere. But wherever I went, even back into the front waiting room, there was nothing.

I frowned at Thirteen and an image from his thoughts slammed into my mind. David Sasser, sitting at a small circular table, sharing drinks with him and Banks.

Oh my God. I knew him.

"He was at the Turtle," I said. "The day of our first meeting. He wasn't in the conference room with us, but he was there, sitting with a group of businessmen having lunch."

Thirteen's thoughts immediately shifted. Heather moaned, "Oh God, he was there?"

Thirteen turned his serious eyes on me again. "Are you sure you can't sense anything?"

"There's nothing," I said again. "Either my family hasn't been here, or they didn't use any power."

"Would they do that? Torture someone without using their powers?"

"No," I said, searching the room again. The slice of hand hung like some morbid ornament off the chair. "Especially with the broken window. The guy, Sasser, would have screamed when they cut off his hand. They would have needed a camouflage to cover what they were doing. Even in this neighborhood. But there's just nothing here."

Thirteen rubbed his hand up and down Heather's arm while she shook against his chest. Once again I found myself questioning Thirteen's choice of team members.

"Heather?" he asked softly, gently pulling her away from him. "What is it, exactly, that has you so upset? You've seen body parts before…"

Heather choked on a sob and kept her eyes closed. It took her a couple of tries to find her voice. "There's just so much hate. It's everywhere. How could someone do that to another human being? All that blood and pain. It's just so horrible." She curled again into Thirteen's chest.

All that blood and pain? Come on. The hand was pretty gross, I guess, but there wasn't really even that much blood.

I met Thirteen's gaze and, even though he didn't think it, I got the distinct impression he wanted me to look inside Heather's mind.

I reached out to her thoughts and had to step back. The sheer openness of her mind was overwhelming. She wasn't just cringing from the severed fingers on the chair—she was cringing from every evil act that had taken place in this building. She couldn't see visions of actual people being tortured, but she felt their pain. As well as the hatred that had caused that pain.

And I recognized the hatred that she sensed. I still didn't feel any residual power in the room, but the intensity and depth of the evil she felt was like a homecoming for me. Oh, my family had been here all right. Maybe not this time, with this guy, but they had used this building. And often.

A wave of violent tremors shook Heather. Her empathic abilities had her so scared and confused—no wonder Thirteen had kept her from crime scenes.

"We should be going," Thirteen said.

I nodded absently, then followed as he led Heather back to the car. I locked the alley door behind me and waited on the curb as Thirteen laid Heather down in the backseat. Once the car door was shut, he walked over to me.

"My family didn't torture David Sasser in there," I said before he could ask. "But they did others. She felt it all, even though the lingering power had faded too much for me to sense, she still felt what had been done in there."

Thirteen ran a hand through his hair and looked back at the car. "I shouldn't have brought her. She's too raw. Too sensitive for these things."

I frowned. "If she's going to be on this task force, she's going to see horrible things. That's just the way it is with my family. I'm surprised she hasn't sensed things like this before."

"We try to protect her," Thirteen explained. "Jon especially. If he could, he would get her to leave the Network, but she *has* to help. Has to do her part for the greater good."

I didn't get it. Why did she put herself through this? Especially when she didn't even understand why she felt the things she did.

Thirteen got in the car, and I followed without argument. I closed the door and turned to check on Heather. She'd stopped crying and was just lying on her side on the backseat. Her thoughts were swirling, but always came back to Jon. The very thought of his arms around her calmed her somehow.

I thought of Theo. A warmth filled me as I pictured his five o'clock shadow, the masculine tendons of his neck and the way they flexed. Was this comfort? Probably not. I doubted I'd be blushing this much if it were comfort.

It didn't really matter anyway. However intense this thing between us was, he would never feel that all-encompassing love like Jon felt for Heather. At least not for me.

"Why does your family do such terrible things?"

Heather's voice was quiet. I started to turn away.

"I'm serious," she said a little louder. "I want to know because, truly, I don't understand it. Why do they hurt people so badly?"

I looked in her eyes and saw the scope of her naïveté.

"Because we're evil, Heather."

From the corner of my eye I saw Thirteen flinch. Heather sniffed, but she nodded for me to continue.

"None of us ever met Grandfather, but Grandmother said that's where the power came from. She was the drive behind the

Kelch empire from day one. I'm pretty sure Grandmother was a sociopath. She wanted everyone to either fear her or desire her. She took Grandfather's powers to a whole new level of malevolence with her sons. She trained them, pounded into their heads that they were superior because of their *gifts*. And pain? That was her way to both punish and reward: if Uncle Max did something wrong, he was tortured. If he did something right, Father was.

"She might not have had any powers of her own, but I can tell you that she was the worst of any of us. Couple that with Grandfather's powers and what else can you expect? Pain and torture is all we've ever known."

Heather's eyes were blank, just staring at me. Part of me wanted to peek in her mind again and see her real reaction. But I didn't. Truth was, I didn't want to know how different I looked to her now.

I turned back in my seat and put in my iPod earplugs. Somehow, the sun's uncomfortable glare felt very appropriate for the drive home.

CHAPTER 18

The double beep of the alarm pulled me awake. It had been one month and one day since I'd moved into my little farmhouse, and my dreams were worse than ever. Exhausting. So intense with the reds and golds. Much more of this and I'd have to start adding coffee to my morning whiskey.

I stretched my neck and peered at the bedside clock: 4:30 a.m. Yesterday's training had gone long, so waking up now meant I'd had about five hours of fitful sleep. Not bad, but definitely not enough.

I dragged myself out of bed and stumbled my way to the kitchen. I was dropping ice in my whiskey when Jon and Theo rushed through the front door, Shane and Thirteen right on their heels. Instantly I tensed. Theo and Jon had made copies of their old house keys. Well, wasn't that nice to know.

"What's going on?" I asked.

No one answered. They didn't even acknowledge my presence. They were too busy pushing on floorboards and moving around paintings. Thirteen even removed the sill from under one of the large windows.

I threw back another drink and let the burn wake me up. As each man rummaged through the room, serious weapons were exposed. Guns, ammo, knives, and that was just what I could make out from the kitchen. I'd wondered why a Network Headquarters didn't actually have any Network stuff in it. Apparently, artillery storage had been this place's primary purpose before I showed up. I peered around the kitchen. What else was hidden in my small house?

"Hey!" I shouted. "What the hell is going on?"

Theo looked up at me while he loaded a long-barreled shotgun. Thirteen stepped in front of him, his own large gun held in both hands.

"Banks is gone," he said. "He didn't call in for the three thirty check, and when Chang tried to contact him at home the line had been disconnected." Thirteen cocked his rifle with a loud, terrifying sound. "I went by there personally and found his door completely splintered. Only the doorknob's brass was left. The rest of his house was in order, but there was blood in his bedroom."

My stomach dropped. My family had Banks. Suddenly all the other Network abductions seemed much more real. Thirteen turned back to the disjointed windowsill and gathered more ammo.

"So what exactly are you going to do?" I asked. The high of a coming fight burned in their eyes. For some reason, I couldn't think clearly enough to check if their thoughts were rational.

"We're going to get him back," Shane said and swung a second long gun with a leather strap over his shoulder. "We're going to the estate and we are going to get him back."

Yeah, OK, definitely not thinking rationally.

"Uh, no, you're not," I said.

"No, Shane," Thirteen said at the same time. "That's not what we're doing."

Jon moved to get in Thirteen's face. "Then what the hell are we doing?" he yelled. "We won't wait for Banks's body to show up weeks from now after being tortured in some supernatural way. We're getting him back. Now!"

Thirteen stood at his full height, his jaw set. *Whoa.* Jon didn't back down.

"To break into the Kelch estate now would be suicide," Thirteen said. "We aren't ready to fight them. We don't know the layout of the private lands. At this point, *we* would be more likely to get arrested than one of the brothers. It would be counterproductive to go in there now."

Theo cut in. "Then what are we going to do?"

Thirteen kept his eyes on Jon. "We are going back to Banks's house. We don't know for certain that he was taken back to the estate, but if we can find a trail that leads us in the general direction, we'll have a better chance of finding him before it's too late."

Jon glared at Thirteen. "Fine."

They all turned and started to walk out.

"Aren't you coming?"

Was that a thud from my jaw hitting the floor? "What?"

"If Banks was taken by supernatural force, we won't be able to find any traces of a trail to follow. You're the only one who would recognize it."

"Can I change?" I asked.

"There's no time," Jon called from the front door. "We have to be back here before dawn to brief the others and figure out what to do next. So just move it already!"

So much for a nice little "please join us on tonight's mission" moment. I threw back the rest of my whiskey, tightened the drawstring on my pajama shorts, slipped on my flip-flops, and we were on our way.

...

We rode together in Thirteen's SUV, the extra weapons stored in the back. Fuzzy images of Banks kept flashing through my mind. His meaty hands, that metal eye patch—pieces of someone I knew. And now my family had him. I shifted in my seat. Turned up Korn on my iPod. It didn't help. I was still uncomfortable.

Of course, it didn't help either that I sat bitch between Jon and Shane. Theo had insisted on sitting shotgun.

I had no clue where Banks's house was. We passed a street sign that probably said where we were, but Shane shot me such a glare that I turned away. *OK...I'll just look out Jon's window, then.*

Thirteen wound the car through side streets lined with pear trees. Pristine turn-of-the-century homes sat on wide manicured lawns. Thirteen pulled up to the curb in front of a line of dark brick brownstones. Each townhouse stood three stories high with cement steps that led to the front door. And the doors were exactly alike—thick, chiseled glass with iron detailing.

Except, of course, for the one with its glass door splintered into a thousand tiny pieces.

We parked under an old-fashioned lamppost, or at least one that was made to look old-fashioned. The warm gold light mixed with the bright silvery moonlight to create an eerie glow along the sidewalk. The instant I stepped out of the car I felt it. The fog of power was everywhere. It felt amazing: tingly and warm. For a moment I closed my eyes and just savored the familiarity.

"We have to hurry," Thirteen said. "The police are on their way. One of the Network dispatchers rerouted the call, but it won't take long before they arrive. We've got maybe five minutes, tops."

"Can anyone else feel that?" I asked. The air was so much thicker than before, surely the others felt it too.

"What? The mosquitos?" Shane said, smacking a bug on his forearm. "Who can't feel the little bloodsuckers?"

"No, the…this misty, foggy stuff. Can anyone else feel that?"

"I don't think so," Jon said. "What does it feel like?"

"My family was here," I explained. "Whoever it was definitely used power I'm familiar with, but it doesn't…I can't tell who."

"Can you follow it?" Theo asked. "Tell which direction Banks was taken?"

"I can feel it all over the sidewalk." I looked around but there was nothing to actually see. "I guess if we just keep walking around I'll be able to feel when it disappears."

"First, let's check the house," Thirteen said and led the way up the front steps to Banks's splintered front door. The door had had a dark cherry frame and the glass had been etched with the same exquisite detail that was still evident on his neighbors' homes.

"Did Banks have money?" I asked. I didn't know how much the Network paid, but since Thirteen lived on the same block as my previous safe house I knew that he, at least, didn't live like *this*.

"Earlier in the year he came into an inheritance," Thirteen answered. We stepped carefully through what remained of the door and entered an elaborate foyer with high ceilings and an ornate chandelier. The floor was black-and-white checkered and classical artwork covered so much of the room I could barely make out the color of the wall paint.

"The blood was found in the bedroom," Thirteen whispered and motioned us to the wide antique stair. The artwork continued along the staircase. Maybe there weren't really walls at all. Maybe the home was simply held up by the paintings' frames. We climbed twenty steps to a long, narrow landing at the second floor, then another twenty steps to the third.

No one spoke and no one turned on the lights. The two went hand in hand somehow. All the while, I felt the same silky fog on my skin, as if the energy circled me as I walked.

The stairs ran out at the third floor, ending where a set of double doors opened to Banks's bedroom. We walked hesitantly into the room. A very large four-poster bed, high enough to need a step stool, faced the doorway. The bedding was rumpled, but the rest of the room seemed in order. On the far wall was a wide fireplace with no screen. The exposed bricks rose from the hearth to the ceiling. This was the only part of the house I'd seen where the walls weren't hidden behind an endless array of artwork.

"The blood is over here," Jon said, crouching by the fireplace.

I met Thirteen next to Jon and looked down at the blood. *That's it? Seriously?* It was just a couple of drops on the carpet. The others crouched beside Jon. They might have been doing some important data gathering, but it looked just like staring to me. I bent down beside them, finding a space between Shane and Thirteen.

"Do you still feel the foggy stuff from outside?" Shane asked me in a hushed voice.

"Yeah, it's all over the place in here." I reached out and ran my finger through the blood.

"What the hell are you doing?"

"Don't touch it!"

"What do you think you're doing?!"

And a barrage of other words and thoughts snapped at me in whispered yells. Theo grabbed my hand. For a moment I held my breath—now was *so* not the time for some supernatural reaction to his touch. Fortunately, the urge was manageable. A longing still flared inside of me—his touch so warm and firm—but there was no burst of energy. No disturbing images or feelings.

"You can't touch the blood, Mag," he said softly. "It's evidence. We can't tamper in any way with a crime scene. Ever."

My face burned. I jerked my hand from his grip.

"I wanted to see if I could tell anything by it," I hissed. "The power is so much stronger here. I figured if it was blood from my family, I'd feel it."

"So was it?" Shane asked.

My cheeks burned hotter. "I can't tell."

We stood in a tight broken circle around the bloodstains. The gray moonlight was fading fast, the sky more purple now than black. Dawn was coming. Along with the police. The Network might work alongside the regular law enforcement when necessary, but the whole secret agency thing kinda made it a strained relationship.

Thirteen motioned us back to the stairs. "We got the confirmation we needed—one of the Kelches was definitely here in Banks's room. Let's head back outside and see if we can get a sense for anything more before we head out."

Thankfully, no one said anything more about my CSI faux pas. We headed down the stairs single file, me taking up the rear. As the sky brightened, the images in the artwork became more apparent. Flashes of bright colors swam around us. Moving, swirling, almost alive. I watched the steps, clutched the railing, tried to avoid looking at the walls.

Outside, I took a steadying breath. Thirteen motioned me over to where he stood in the shadows around the streetlight. "I need you to walk up and down the sidewalk until you no longer feel the energy that you feel now."

I nodded and moved in exaggerated steps down the sidewalk. The misty energy tingled along my skin. After a few steps, I felt like an idiot walking so deliberately, so I just strolled normally.

Just before reaching the first neighbor, the tingling lightened then pulled away. I took one more step forward then one more back just to be sure I felt the difference.

"Right here. I don't feel it anymore over here."

"That's not real far," Jon pointed out.

"Try the other direction, Magnolia," Thirteen said from his place in the shadows.

This time I walked two houses down before the feeling started to fade. Instinctively, I moved toward the curb. The fogginess abruptly disappeared.

"I think they got in a car, because it's just suddenly gone here at the curb."

Thirteen nodded thoughtfully. "OK," he said. "Come back and let's get back to HQ."

We filed back into Thirteen's car. Thirteen spoke quietly from the driver's seat. "What use of power would be necessary from the sidewalk, all through the house, and back outside?"

There was a long pause. Thirteen peered at me from the rear-view mirror.

"Oh!" Guess that wasn't rhetorical. "Probably just a camouflage illusion. Unless, well, who called the police?"

"I did," Thirteen said. "I reported the break-in on our way over here."

"Then they definitely used a camouflage. You know, it's like an illusion to cover themselves, make everything appear normal so none of the neighbors would see what was really happening."

"But would that mask the sound?" asked Shane. "I mean, that door was shattered, exploded. Surely someone heard that."

I nodded. "They probably did hear something, but if there was nothing to see to go with the sound, then..."

"You can do that?" Jon asked. "Explode a door without anyone knowing you did it?"

"Sure," I said. "As long as they were there to hold the illusion. They could have even talked to the neighbors and no one would have known what happened. It's just like what you guys have been training on. Of course, if it were me, I wouldn't even need a camouflage illusion. I'd just turn invisible, unlock the door, and make any bodies I was hauling with me invisible too. Then there wouldn't be any threat of discovery at all. The others can't do that, though, so even if they were doing an illusion, which I can pretty much guarantee they were, it would be hard for them to cover a sound and a body at the same time. Especially one as big as Banks."

Silence filled the car. All eyes were on me; the men's faces turned hard.

OK, what did I do now?

I quickly peeked in their minds. *Shit.* "I didn't mean like a *body* body! Like I'd carry out a *dead* body," I spoke in a rush. "Banks probably isn't even dead yet. He had to be able to walk out on his own, right? Since they wouldn't have been able to camouflage his appearance at the same time they were covering the door and themselves and who knows what else. So I didn't mean he's really a *body* body. Not like that."

"No," growled Shane, "he's not dead yet. He's just being tortured at some unknown location. That's all."

Everyone turned forward again. Great.

Chapter 19

I sat alone on the front porch and watched the sun set. Training had been canceled again so everyone could have a catch-up day at the office. In order to keep my involvement secret from the rest of the Network, Thirteen had made everything about the task force confidential. Which was fine, except that confidentiality meant the folks on our team were now forced to do research and paperwork they would have otherwise pawned off to other staff members.

I, for one, was glad for the day off. Things were so…strange right now. Banks was gone. They knew who had him, but with no physical proof their hands were tied. Everyone was on edge. Conversations were snarled rather than spoken. People were as quick to throw a punch as a sarcastic retort. Hell, the other day Charles had even asked to up the combat training just so everyone could work out some of the frustration.

But that wasn't all.

I was changing. I didn't know how or why, but at my very core, I was…evolving. I could feel it as certainly as I could feel the hot evening air.

I jumped up and walked out into the yard. I couldn't just sit here anymore. My pace quickened until I was running past the wide back field. Faster and faster I moved. The trees tore at my clothes but I didn't care. I hadn't run like this since my escape. It felt good to feel the wind gain speed around me. Free. I'd never been in control of my life. But now, recently, I wasn't even in control of *me*. Intense dreams. Unexpected powers. Theo. All these… feelings.

I couldn't run fast enough.

Night fell quickly. Before I knew it, I was several miles from the farmhouse. *Shit.* I wound through the trees, following the sound of cars on a busy road. When I could see the street, I recognized it from my trip to Target. No wonder I had a cramp—I'd just run about twenty miles in ten minutes. With deep breaths, I walked along the road back to my farmhouse, staying under the cover of trees and bushes. The return trip took much longer.

At least my run had served its purpose: by the time I got home, I was too exhausted to think anymore. My Target-brand sheets and quilt welcomed me with cool comfort. On the bed, I curled on my side and sighed. My flowing yellow curtains waved me good night right before I closed my eyes and passed out.

• • •

Everything was red. Painful, pulsing red. It felt like an ax had lodged itself right in the middle of my forehead, splitting my skull in two. This wasn't one of my normal dreams. It was too painful.

I took a deep breath, hoping to ease some of the pain. A rancid stench filled my lungs—mildew mixed with blood and grain.

I flinched and the rub of restraints burned against my ankles and wrists. *Oh God.* It was all too familiar not to recognize.

No, no, no, no! This could not be happening. It *had* to be a dream. But the pain was too real to deny.

I was back.

Somehow, some way, they had gotten through the Network defenses, past my own senses, and dragged me back to the estate. I strained to peel open my eyes. When I did, a wave of nausea overwhelmed me. My stomach turned over. My throat burned, and the smell was enough to make me heave again. I leaned forward, gagging.

I pulled at my arms. Just like my eyes, moving was a forced effort. My body wasn't working right.

There was a sound. It must have been ongoing, but I only noticed it now. Some kind of low grinding. A machine of some sort. No voices, no cars in the near distance. *Shit.*

The walls were dark and powdered with dried dirt and ancient grain. The reinforced ceiling, a large square window, the thick metal door in front of me. I hadn't been in here since I was child, but I knew where I was: the farthest silo on the southern acres. It was rusted to the point of crumbling. To the left of the door was a desk with a table lamp turned on. And next to the lamp sat my guard—a small, dark-haired man in a disheveled gray suit… sleeping. His snores were the low grinding I heard. His collared shirt was unbuttoned nearly halfway down his hollow chest and his feet hung off the end of the desk. Thin and lanky—was this a joke? My head not restrained, a nothing guard—*What the hell was going on?*

I closed my eyes as a wave of dizziness overtook me. With a deep breath, I stretched against my restraints and felt leather bite into my wrists.

Wait a minute. *Leather straps? Were they serious?* Only thick chains were ever strong enough to hold me. I pulled again, but my arm barely moved under the leather.

The guard shifted in his sleep, and suddenly he wasn't the dark-haired, skinny man anymore. He wasn't a man at all. He was a woman, her blonde hair pulled back into a tight ponytail, stretching her already sharp features. Alabaster skin spotted with dark, scabbed lesions covered her sickly frame. A torn and stained halter top accented the knobs of bone in her shoulders, and her shredded jean shorts were cut too short to leave anything to the imagination.

Terror consumed me. I couldn't breathe. The woman turned her sunken face toward me. "Teddy?" she asked in a heavy whisper. "Teddy Bear, is that you?"

Images slashed through my mind. Foreign, haunting scenes of a life before I was put in foster care, before I found Jon and the others, before I won a scholarship to Butler and became a decorated Navy SEAL. A life before the Network—a life with a mother, the hooker who raised me on the streets of Chicago.

I squeezed my eyes shut. *Please, please no!*

The guard coughed and grumbled then returned to the rhythm of his heavy snores. I peeked through my lids again and the scrawny man was back, still sleeping soundly with his head back against the wall.

What…the fuck…was that?

I pulled against the leather straps hard this time, but again, my arms barely lifted at all. Drugs could explain the hallucinations and the nausea, but what was with this weakness? Maybe there was a chain-linked interior to the straps or something…

I stopped. The leather had cut into my wrist—a tanned, thick wrist that led to a firm, calloused hand with blunt nails and a thin scar across the knuckles.

This wasn't my hand.

My mind worked furiously. This was not my body, not my memories. It was not *me* being held here. It was only a piece of my mind in this horrific place.

Relief washed over me. Wherever I was, I was safe from this nightmare. But this body and mind were not. Whoever had been captured and brought to this place, he didn't have my powers to free himself or to recover from whatever torture awaited. And I was here in his mind, experiencing it with him.

I concentrated on separating my voice from his to hear those thoughts that weren't my own. The collage of profanity in this man's mind rang through, more impressive than anything I had ever heard. This guy was seriously pissed and seriously scared. Strangely, the thought of the emaciated woman returning frightened him more than any possible torture that was sure to come.

He just didn't know any better.

The snoozing guard stirred again. We had to get out of here. Like, now. With a deep breath, I reached out with my thoughts.

Um, calm down, please. I want to get you out of here.

Silence. Great. Maybe if I just tried to focus on this guy's thoughts rather than trying to speak with mine...

What the hell is wrong with me? I'm hearing fucking voices now? What the fuck did they give me?

Thank God. I tried again with my most soothing voice. *Please, I'm not part of the drugs, but you have to let me help you get out of here.*

Fuck that! These fuckers are going to pay for even thinking they could mess with my head!

OK, this wasn't working.

Centering on his right arm, I forced my will and strength into his body. In a fast, smooth movement I pulled the wrist free from the leather binding without leaving so much as a burn on his skin.

See, I can get you out of here if you'll just shut up and listen to me!

There was a long pause. *Mag?*

My thoughts scattered. The coined nickname, the sudden warm and violent fluttering inside me—how could I have not known? My family had captured Theo. And somehow, through the connection between us, I was with him.

It took several moments for me to compose myself.

I—I can get you out of here, but you have to give me some control.

How the hell am I supposed to do that?

I just pulled your arm free because you didn't fight me. Let me get you free from your restraints, then we'll get the hell out of here.

You know where I am?

Yes.

Movement from the corner caught us off guard. Our snoozing guard was awake. He hopped to the dirt floor with barely a thud and stretched his lanky arms to the ceiling.

While the guard's face was pointed at the ceiling in his stretch, I pulled Theo's other arm and both legs free from their binds with one quick move. He gasped but was quiet enough not to gain the guard's attention.

What the…? Warn me before you do something like that again!

Sorry.

The guard shot us a glance then looked steadily at his watch, counting the minutes to the next shift change. Suddenly his appearance changed again. From my mind's eye I knew the man was still peering down at his watch, still calculating. But through

Theo's eyes the disturbing blonde woman was back, and her black eyes looked wild as her gaze met ours.

"Teddy Bear!" her voice scratched like broken glass. "You listen to me and get your skinny ass down there like Sonny said. Do you want to go back in the coal room?"

Theo froze in horror.

A protective impulse sprang to life inside me. I focused an angry surge of power from my consciousness into Theo's, clearing his head and evaporating the hallucination. The small guard was still looking at his watch. No more than a couple of seconds had passed.

Then the guard turned his full attention to us. A slow, creepy smile spread across his face, revealing a mouth full of stained little teeth.

It was his last expression.

Theo moved like a natural predator. Fluid. His lunge was beautiful, smooth and fast in a way that seemed choreographed. And watching him move through his own eyes, I saw how automatic his grace was, how disciplined and confident…and deadly. The skinny man was dead on his feet before he knew we were out of the chair.

Theo gently laid the man on the dirt floor and began scanning for cameras and other security. I wasn't sure if I was more impressed by his gentleness or his fierceness. Either way, I was totally getting hot.

They know something's happened. Theo thought. *They're turning on some kind of furnace or something.*

Oops.

Er, no, the only camera is on the other side of the door. The wire is exposed at the doorframe.

The last thing I needed from him was more attitude so I didn't force his eyes upward to where the wire was obviously visible. He'd barely started to scan the doorframe when he turned a sudden about-face and ran to the desk. Quickly he rummaged through the drawers.

Um, we're kind of in a hurry here.

He ignored me. In the second drawer he found it: a long horseshoe pritchel. Twelve inches long, it was thicker than an ice pick and sharper on its tip. It had dried blood thick on the length of its shaft. Theo held it up to the light, examining it as he rotated his wrist back and forth. He held it like he should—like a weapon. Watching him in all his seductive, predatory glory set off my butterflies.

The wire, I reminded him.

Instantly, he was back at the door. He glanced over the exposed cable twice before he saw it. With his fast fingers—not the time to ponder that fact too closely—he disabled the camera. In a matter of seconds we were poised at the door to make our escape.

Wait, I cautioned. *They always keep someone on guard outside. I'm going to need to listen. Do you* mind *if I use your ears?*

His eyes rolled and a wave of dizziness rocked our balance.

OK, don't do that again.

Well don't be so damn patronizing!

Great, more attitude.

Are you going to let me listen or not?

His arm waved in an impatient response—my sign to go ahead. He leaned closer to the door, not realizing that it wasn't necessary. Once he turned over control of his ears, I could hear the stale conversation of the yard crew on the southern acres, and then, farther, voices of those in the main house.

All at once my heart stopped. Father was here, inside the main house. I could hear him snapping orders to one of the servants. His voice scraped along the inside of my mind, paralyzing every other thought. Theo froze, sharing in my terror. I could feel the hair on the back of his neck stand on end.

What's happening?

I couldn't respond, couldn't even think. The horrors of my life were too close. *Please don't let them know I'm alive.* I felt the words more than thought them.

Mag. Theo's thoughts were stern. *Mag, I need you to focus. I'm not going to let them do anything to us, do you understand? Just show me the way out and we will leave this place.*

It took a full minute, and everything I had, to turn away from my father's voice.

OK, I finally responded. *There's no one outside the door, but security guards monitor the cameras so we only have a few minutes before someone comes to check on the disabled wires.*

Theo tucked the horseshoe pick in his waistband and used both hands to grip the large dead bolt. With a heave he cranked open the heavy metal door. There was a small, enclosed area, maybe four feet by four feet with a low sheet metal ceiling and concrete floor. At the end was a second locked door that led to the outside. Theo swung the large metal door closed behind us, locking it in place with a clang. He winced as he turned to the second door. A step forward, then he hissed. Clutching his right shoulder, he fell against one of the unfinished walls. When he brought his hand back down, blood covered it.

You're hurt.

Wherever my body was, it had stopped breathing. Fear, worry, guilt—I was consumed by the thought of someone tearing into Theo's body they way they had mine so many times. How stupid could I be? Assuming that when I had awoken in his mind, his time as a captive had just started. I should have known better.

What did they do to you? What did they want to know?

I don't remember, he thought and clutched his shoulder tighter. I could feel him trying to recall what happened, but his thoughts were fuzzy, disjointed from the drugs.

Don't worry about it now. We need to get out of here.

He nodded absently. Now that the pain had surfaced he was weaker, but his determination was incredible.

OK, what do I do?

On the other side of the door will be two paths. One leads to the horse barns and the other leads into the woods that circle the estate. Take the trail on the right into the woods. I don't know if it's night or day, so you'll need the tree cover.

Theo nodded. He put his back against the wall. He peered from the side, the pritchel back in his left hand as he opened the door with his right. As the door cracked open, a sliver of gray light shone in the dark room. There was no movement or sound in the immediate area—only the chirp of crickets and the buzz of mosquitoes to fill our ears.

Theo opened the door wider. The moon shone brightly, high in the sky among a million stars. Silently, Theo moved. From the silo to the woods, he disappeared into the night. I knew the landscape well, but moving with Theo brought with it a whole new excitement. His grace and intensity were intoxicating. Once inside the tree line, he stopped against a thick maple, taking a moment to breathe through the pain of his injuries.

What had they done to him?

Without the benefit of my own eyes I couldn't explore his body to see the severity of his injuries. And he was trained enough to know that looking at your wounds only made the pain worse. So after a couple of heartbeats, he was ready to move again.

Straight ahead until you cross a small creek. You can get a drink and then head west toward the highway.

How far?

About two hundred yards to the stream and another half mile to the road.

It was a haul, but he refused to show any wear. With another deep breath he was off. I stayed quiet while he ran. His movements were so smooth, so quiet, that if I hadn't been with him I would have thought any noise he made was from any other night creature living on the estate. The babbling of the creek, once it hit his ears, made him run faster. Only when the water was in sight did he slow. Just inside the tree line, we paused and listened.

Is there anything?

I listened closely. No one had left the main house, but two of the guards at the security station were talking about the silo camera suddenly shutting off. They were drawing straws to see who would check it out.

They know the camera is broken. They haven't started the cart to head over there yet, but one of the guards is on his way to the maintenance garage. It will take at least seven minutes for him to reach the silo.

Nothing right here, though?

No, but you need to hurry.

Without a sound he moved to the creek. He cupped his hands and drank in the cool water. The refreshment was instantaneous. I couldn't feel the burn of his throat, but I could feel his satisfaction as if it were my own. He rose from the creek without gorging himself, drinking only enough to quench his thirst and keep his head clear. That more than anything else told me about his life. You can be trained to fight and to move and to think on instinct, but only someone who has suffered actual starvation would know his limit before making himself ill with overconsumption.

West? he asked, already moving in that direction.

Yes. It's a way, but just head in a straight line and you will hit the wall before the highway. There are cameras and guards that patrol the wall so I'll let you know when we're close.

It was dark under the trees. The moonlight provided little light through the full branches. He had moved a fast one hundred yards when a black shadow rose between the trees ahead. It was impossible to make out in the darkness, but it appeared to be larger than a human. Thicker. Theo moved in an arc around the shadow.

What is it?

I tried to use his sight to make out the shape. Bigger than a person. A work truck, maybe? We were almost on it before realization hit me, and my mind was paralyzed with terror once more. Theo froze with me. His heart sped up and his silent breath stopped completely as he tensed for a strike.

Danger? It was a feeling inside him rather than an actual thought.

It took more than a couple of heartbeats for me to recover enough to respond.

No. No danger. It's…it's just a shed.

A shed? Then why…?

Just keep going!

He paused a moment longer before survival took precedence over easing my fear and he was moving once again. By the time we were close enough for me to make out the wall patrol I was nearly composed again.

Stop. He stopped. *There's a guard fifty yards away but I can't tell if he's coming or going.*

Theo stood rooted while I listened to the guard's movements.

Moving away. He already passed by here.

Theo took a step forward.

Wait, the wall is covered with cameras. Not a single inch isn't under constant surveillance.

Then how...?

You have to let me take over. The only way past the cameras is for me to create an illusion. I have to have complete control to do that.

Theo tensed. He could not, would not give me complete control of his mind. And how could I blame him? I sure as hell wouldn't have done it. But I truly didn't know of another way to get past the cameras.

He didn't think the words but I could read his distrust clearly: I was a Kelch. This could be a ploy to invade his thoughts and gain access to Network secrets. But then I could have picked anything out of Thirteen's head at any time over the last several months.

The confusion of the bond between us flitted in his thoughts.

His mind shifted. Focusing on our strange connection, his breathing staggered, his stomach clenched. And his reaction only fueled my own.

Mag! Shit. Had I thought that out loud? *Just do it and get us out of here!*

Are you sure?

The moment we are past the wall, that very moment, I want back in. Not a few steps past the wall, not once we get to the highway, but the very instant we are past that wall, I'm back. Agreed?

Absolutely.

He nodded and closed his eyes. With a deep breath, I felt him blank out his thoughts. I slid right in. It was incredible, easy. I had never taken over another person's mind so completely. It was like stepping into someone else's life. His memories, his feelings, his senses—I could sense the core of who he was. Driven and capable, strong and loyal, trained and determined. I could recall every one of his memories, even those he had blocked, but I refused to breach that level of privacy. I could also feel the pain of his injuries and a wave of respect washed over me. His physical control was incredible. It was like wading through the essence of Theo, his soul, almost. And my heart swelled as the bond between us grew even more defined.

I located the cameras hidden among the trees. Instantly, I created a camouflage. The cameras would see nothing more than the stagnant vision of the bare white wall. Then in a leap I moved Theo's sculpted body over the eight feet of brick and stone that enclosed the estate.

I stretched as I landed on padded feet. His muscles flexed and his body pulled at my will, running us just beyond the property line. *God, the way his body moved.* Now that we were safe, I really needed to focus on bringing him back. But maybe I could, just real quick…

I ran my hand down the front of his shirt. His stomach muscles rippled underneath the cloth. I brushed fingertips along the edge of his waistband. What would it feel like to touch the skin there? I shuddered.

OK, enough of this. Our eyes closed and I pulled back from his mind, sliding out just as easily as I had slid in. I felt his thoughts and body pull away and I knew I no longer consumed him like I had.

Theo? I called. Nothing. I didn't feel his presence reemerging. *Theo!*

Was it good for you? His thoughts were an octave lower now. And calmer somehow. Relief poured over me.

Theo, thank God! Are you OK? I couldn't sense you.

He started moving toward the glare of moonlight on the asphalt of the highway, visible just on the other side of the woods.

Oh, I'm good. That was, um, quite an experience. Having you inside me.

Heat crept over me. Something about the way the words sounded in his thoughts made me blush. I was just about to ask what it had felt like for him when suddenly he was just…gone.

Theo? Theo, are you there? "Theo!" The last I cried out loud as I sat straight up in my bed, my new quilt bunched in a pile at my feet.

I was in my bed at the farmhouse. The yellow curtains billowed from the open window. The clock beside my bed read 12:37 a.m.

CHAPTER 20

From the kitchen through the great room, I paced. Had it been real? A dream? *Shit.*

With a burst of purpose I flew out the front door to my car. I jammed the key in the ignition, turned over the engine, shoved the gearshift into reverse—then stopped.

Where were Thirteen and the others? If Theo was really gone, where was the panic? Besides, what was I going to do anyway—drive out to my family's estate and look for Theo along the side of the road? Yeah, right.

With heavy feet I chided myself all the way back to bed. I hadn't even bothered throwing on real clothes. I still wore the same camisole and panties that I'd gone to bed in. These new emotions were going to be the death of me, I just knew it. I pulled the sheet up over my face and sighed.

The monitor beeped twice. My stomach dropped. Tires slowly churned over the gravel drive. The engine shut down. A car door shut quietly and footsteps moved softly to the porch.

The single beep of the alarm made me jump as the front door opened and closed.

I couldn't move. *Theo.* His thoughts were a mess, the energy around him mangled with anger and fear and something else.

Quietly, he moved to the kitchen. Cabinets opened and closed. The small light over the stove flipped on, casting shadows in the hall outside my open bedroom door. I crept from my bed to the doorway. I could see him, leaning with his backside against the table, hovering over the contents of the first aid kit. The rips in his clothes, the blood on his hands, all conducive to my midnight memories.

Memories. Not dreams or fantasies. *Oh God.* What did this mean?

Theo hissed as he fumbled with his sleeve. Suddenly, nothing else mattered.

I went to the sink and pulled out some dish towels and a large glass bowl. I turned on the faucet and the rush of water echoed through the house. His eyes watched my every movement, his gaze hot on my back. I wet the clean towels and filled the bowl with warm water.

When I turned off the faucet, the silence was even louder than before. With a gulp I turned to face him. Time stood still when our eyes met. I carried his gaze until I stood directly in front of him. My hands shook as I lifted the wet towel from the bowl.

I had no clue if he would let me do this. And when I looked up to his face, there was a new darkness there that gave me pause. He knew now just how strong my mental abilities were. It had been a leap of faith for him to trust me while at the estate. The pain of his wounds, the absoluteness of my power, the fact that he'd escaped—his mind struggled to hold onto what was real.

I held the dripping towel up for him to see. He frowned, but after a moment, nodded. I lowered the cloth slowly, brushing it along his shoulder and neck. His eyes shut tight and his body tensed. Gently, I pulled what was left of his shirt away from his back, trying my best to ignore his shivers so I could do what was necessary. What no one had ever done for me when I'd been hurt.

Deep gashes raced across his back. His skin was freckled with the blisters of third-degree burns. The tears in his flesh extended over his upper arms, distorting several tattoos there and criss-crossing in ways I hadn't realized when we were running through the woods. But worst of all was the deep laceration just above his right shoulder blade. Someone had dug into his back with a perforated spear, one with tiny, razorlike teeth along the spear's head. I knew the weapon intimately, as well as the pain it caused.

Seeing his injury, knowing how it was created, a hot anger swelled in my chest. I wanted blood. The demand was like a thirst. Someone needed to bleed for what had been done to him.

But then the shredded skin around the edge of his wound began to ooze a green metallic puss. *Damn it!* The spear had been poisoned. I leaned back on my heels with a curse. I met Theo's gaze. "I can heal it," I whispered.

A million thoughts passed behind his eyes. I could almost see each individual one. Finally, the line of his mouth tightened and he gave a curt nod.

I moved slowly, leaning completely over the side of his body. His heat warmed my face and tensed my body. I could place a hand on his shoulder and it would heal him, but like with Charles, it would be excruciating. Then, I'd cared more about getting the healing over with than the pain it might cause. Now, I didn't want to hurt Theo any more than necessary. So I used my breath.

With the gentlest breeze I could manage, I blew a focused breath across his shoulder and let my power flow over him. I watched as the muscle knitted itself back together. Within seconds, new, shiny skin covered the wound. He shivered but he didn't stop me. I crawled onto the table and curved around him, positioning myself to breathe on the rest of his injuries.

I dipped my head to his waist and caressed his lower back with my breath. I tried to focus on nothing but his wounds, but his skin was so warm, his muscles so tight. And that scent of musk and metal never faded, even with the blood and sweat on top of it. My breath turned to a subtle pant; my low stomach muscles tightened in a wonderfully uncomfortable way. And as my body responded, that electricity—that frustrating bond between us—grew even more pronounced.

Unfamiliar emotions stirred inside me—sudden longings much more demanding than the comfort I'd come to expect when he was near. The butterflies that had sprung to life in my stomach spilled south in a rush. I gasped. My eyes closed. *Oh God. Concentrate.*

Theo's body had been tense since my first breath on his shoulder. But when I blew the last necessary breath on the side of his abdomen, just above the waistband of his fitted jeans, his muscles clenched in a way that they hadn't before, shaking him under their pull. I pulled away quickly.

Theo's back and arms were drenched in sweat. I crawled down from the table and stood by his side. His eyes were closed, but not clenched like they had been. He seemed…calm now. His head tilted to one side, like he was listening to some soothing music.

I stood motionless, watching him. Finally, he rolled his eyes open to look at me. They seemed lighter somehow. He didn't smile, but there was a peace to him that I had never seen.

"Thank you," he breathed, his voice deep.

My entire body lightened at the husky sound of his voice. Behind me the wall clock chimed. One thirty. Exhaustion fell heavy on Theo's shoulders. I watched him hunch over and drag a weary hand over his face.

I reached out until my fingers touched the top of his hand. He turned a fraction and stared at my fingers on top of his.

My hand moved on its own; my fingers curled around his palm and he followed as I somehow led him from the kitchen to my small bedroom. With barely a pause in the doorway, I took him to the bed.

Moonlight peeked through the curtains and cast a shadowed white glow throughout the room. I pulled back my top sheet and fixed my new quilt with my free hand before gently directing Theo to lie down. He kept his eyes on me but let me help him into the bed. Once lowered to his side, I pulled the soft sheet and quilt over him. I wanted to stay. The pull I felt was so strong, it was physically difficult to step away. But I tried anyway. He didn't let go. He held on tighter.

The deep darkness in his eyes had returned, tightening his face. And with it, another emotion I couldn't name. I stood there for a long minute. *What did he want me to do?* His thoughts were jumbled, his wants as confused as mine. My fingers began to tingle from the strength of his grip. Hesitantly, I moved toward the foot of the bed. I had to stretch my arm to keep our hands together. Crawling on hands and knees, I fumbled over his legs and lay beside him. He closed his eyes and tightened his grip, clutching my hand over his heart.

After several motionless minutes, his breathing slowed to the rhythmic rumble of sleep. His scent surrounded me. I sighed and let my body curve into his. It felt so good to be wrapped around him, but I couldn't relax. I let my mind wander as I held him in the darkness.

CHAPTER 21

I hadn't heard them coming. Father and Uncle Max had been traveling—a brief reprieve for me. I had even watched some TV before drifting off to sleep. Malcolm and Markus had taken advantage, of course, but a quick snap of Malcolm's forearm had gained me some down time. Markus would never come after me alone.

I woke screaming, reaching for my legs. There was only blood. My knees were gone, shattered. Father was back and he stood beside the bed, a sledgehammer resting on his shoulder. My vision blurred from the pain as I struggled to breathe. I couldn't feel anything below my hips.

"Listen to him!" Father shouted at me.

I blinked several times, trying to focus. Other men's thoughts swirled around me. But I couldn't breathe, couldn't see. God, my legs! Father's hand stung as it slapped across my face.

"I said, listen to him!"

Two guards stood like a wall at Father's back. Thick and drugged, their minds rarely saw past their orders. But this time there was something real there—fear. Between them was a man. Bloody, beaten, barely conscious. Welcome to the club. *His hands were restrained behind his back. He sat heavy on his knees, on the brink of passing out. A moan escaped his lips. "Can't..."*

Father's boot slammed into the man's side. He moved so fast I missed it. He turned to me again. "Do it, damn it! Listen to him!"

For I moment my mind blanked. Father wanted something from me. Something real and useful—to listen to this man's thoughts and find something specific. Against my will a strange warmth rose inside me.

I shut down the feeling immediately. Where was Uncle Max?

The guards shifted and their thoughts grew clear. This was the last survivor of a terrorist family who had inadvertently stolen the wrong plane. They had thought they were hijacking drugs. They had ended up with guns. Weapons en route to a foreign dignitary Uncle Max was trying to woo. The rest of his family was here. Or they had been before Uncle Max had spent the day with them. But Uncle Max couldn't breach this man's mind. He'd literally worn himself out of power.

Father dragged the man over to the bed and tossed him on top of me. His body sprawled over my broken legs. A wave of pain shot up my spine. I gasped. Father picked the sledgehammer back up.

"Wha-what do you need me to find?"

He hesitated with the enormous mallet poised to swing. "Where are our guns?" His growled words were not human. Not at all.

Matted, bloody hair hid the man's face. But through the blood, he lifted his head and met my eyes. Oh...no. He didn't know. He'd told them he didn't know. Over and over. But they hadn't believed him, not without Uncle Max confirming it.

I took a deep breath and stamped down the pain. No point in dwelling on it now. There would only be more.

Sitting as straight as possible, I looked at Father. "He doesn't know."

His anger swelled through the room. The mirror shattered. The bed shook. For a terrifying moment he questioned my honesty. But he dismissed the thought quickly. After all, why would I lie?

As quickly as his anger had appeared, he reined it in. He smoothed back his dark hair, brushed off his sleeves, returned to the disciplined posture he gave the public eye. With a sniff, he looked down on the crumpled man once more. Then he turned for the door.

Was that it? He wasn't going to slam that sledgehammer into my skull? Or use one of those pocketknives he always carried to "kill" the messenger?

At the door, he paused. I tensed. Here it comes. He flicked his wrist and the man's neck snapped. His shuddering body became dead weight on my legs. But his head kept turning. The bones of his neck cracked and scraped until his head was turned at a completely unnatural angle, his open eyes staring right at me.

One of the guards stepped forward. "No," Father commanded. "Leave him."

Then he turned and left the room. And the two guards followed, shutting the door behind them. The man's body was heavy on my shins—just far enough away that I couldn't reach him without moving my lower body. And Father had made damn sure that wasn't going to happen.

So we'd spent the night like that. Me alive, wishing I was dead. And Father's terrorist, lying on top of me, his dead eyes unable to look away.

...

There was no fear or nausea lying with Theo. No pain. Just… calm. My hand was still clasped over his heart. His steady snores faltered. I held my breath as he slowly stretched his body.

Relaxing again, he rubbed his hands over his face and rolled onto his back. Eyes still closed, he moved his hand to his chest and felt around like he was searching for something. I flexed my hand to regain some circulation and his eyes popped open. Immediately, he saw my hand and grabbed it like a lifeline. Only when my palm was clutched once more over his heart did he settle back on the bed.

"How are you feeling?" I whispered.

"I'm good…I think. Sore, but good." His voice was rough from sleep. "I didn't know you could do that. Enter someone's mind like that from a distance."

I swallowed. "I didn't know I could do that either. I—I've never done anything like that before. I wasn't sure it was even real until you showed up here like that."

He just stared at me. I cleared my throat and asked, "How did you get here? I couldn't, um, sense you anymore after you made it to the highway. How did you get back to your car?"

He looked down at where our joined hands rested on his chest. Softly, he rubbed his thumb across the backs of my knuckles.

"I'd made it about a mile on the highway," he said, "when there was a guy being pulled over for drunk driving. The cop had him out of the car and doing the sobriety test. I waited until he arrested the guy and left the car for a tow truck. I hotwired it and drove it here. I figured I'd return it to the address on the registration."

"You can hotwire a car?"

"You learn to develop your own special abilities working for the Network."

The sun threatened morning light and I could see him a little better now. His eyes looked tired, but still alert—like somehow the predator in him never really went to sleep. His hand looked huge on top of mine and his continuous rubbing turned more into a caress.

"It was like you were right there with me," he said softly. "I could hear you as if you were right next to me. And when you moved, I could actually feel you inside me." He frowned again. "You've really never done anything like that before?"

My voice stuck in my throat. The way his fingers felt on my hand, I couldn't help but picture them caressing other parts of me as well. What was his question?

I swallowed twice, then finally said, "I've been in people's heads before, but I've never been inside someone so...completely before. Not ever."

He nodded. I wanted to move closer to him but wasn't sure if that would shut down this new openness between us. How could a feeling so strong seem so fragile?

"Why did you do it, then?" he asked. "I mean, did...did you know they were going to take me?"

Ice exploded in my chest, stealing my breath. The accusation was like a physical blow, only worse. I yanked my hand away. With both hands he snatched it back.

"I didn't know you were taken until I was in your head!" I snapped. "And even then, I didn't know it was *you*, not at first. I just fell asleep and woke up tied to that chair."

"OK," he said quickly, pulling me back toward him. "OK, I believe you."

And he did. With absolute certainty, he believed me. So when both his thumbs began rubbing lightly from my fingers to my wrist, I let him. After a few minutes, I settled back into his side.

A few minutes more and it was like the pierce of his words had never happened. All I could feel was his hand on mine.

"So why *do* you think you were able to get in my head?" He studied my face. "Why me?" he whispered.

"I don't know," I whispered back. "You were drugged. Maybe that opened your mind to me, allowed me to slip in. Or maybe it was something else."

We lay there in silence for a long while, just looking at each other.

"That was your mother, wasn't it?" I finally whispered. "The woman that you saw?"

His thumbs froze midmassage. *Crap.* Why the hell didn't I just keep my mouth shut?

"Never mind," I said quickly. "It's none of my business."

"It's OK," he said. "Yeah, that was my mom. I never saw her look that bad, though. She died when I was fifteen. I hadn't seen her for years."

"I'm sorry."

"Don't be. It's not your fault. Hell, it wasn't even her fault. Her family turned her into that."

"What do you mean?"

He took a deep breath. "My mother was sixteen when she got pregnant by her dealer. Her dad was a Chicago bigwig in retail and couldn't handle the scandal. So instead of sending her to rehab or getting her an abortion, they just threw her out. She had me and we lived with her dealer until social services found me and put me in foster care."

His thumbs started moving again.

"I looked up her family once when I was ten," he continued. "They live in some mansion outside the city. You should see the house—all decked out in European columns and trellises. They even have this scrolled iron sign in some old-world language at the gate to their driveway, showing off their culture and heritage. It was all so different from where I lived…it wasn't like anything you went through—not by a long shot—but it wasn't a fun life."

He closed his eyes and pulled on my hand, drawing me into his side until my cheek rested on his shoulder. He took a deep breath and I sensed a release in him, like he was somehow lighter now. He turned his face into my hair and sighed.

I was tired too. And lighter. Like talking with Theo had somehow removed something from both of us. Or maybe shifted the weight of it. A strange awareness slowly dawned on me as I lay there. Maybe somehow, with Theo, maybe I could forget the evil that lived inside me. Maybe I could actually forget that I was a Kelch. Maybe together…

Theo opened his eyes. My thoughts scattered. He was so close. When he took a deep breath, our cheeks brushed. His lips parted and I closed my eyes. The contours of my body fit perfectly against his. So warm, so safe. His hand moved against my hip and I slid even closer, searching. My own lips parted so I could taste his breath on my tongue. He lowered his face.

The double beep of the alarm sounded.

We froze.

CHAPTER 22

Theo cursed under his breath and lifted himself to stand. He swayed on his feet, then fell right back down on the bed.

"Stay here," I said softly. "You need more than just a couple of hours of sleep."

He wanted to argue, but he was completely drained. With a light push I got him to lie back down. I crawled from the bed and grabbed a T-shirt and cotton shorts. As I pulled them on, my faced burned. I had healed Theo, spent the night lying next to him, just had that unbelievable moment against him, and the whole time I wore nothing but ugly purple panties and a faded green camisole top. I didn't even want to think about what my hair looked like.

In the kitchen, I poured myself a drink. Would Theo want one? Or maybe coffee? He probably didn't drink whiskey for breakfast like me. I started up the coffee pot when the monitor beeped again. Jon fumbled at the door before he and Shane charged into the house. Thirteen's large form moved quickly in their wake.

"We want answers and we want them now!" Shane roared as soon as he saw me.

I shifted my weight, adjusting my grip on the whiskey bottle. Shane drew up short. Confusion and anger shaded all their thoughts.

"You have to know more than you're telling us, Magnolia," Jon said evenly. He stood across the table from me and leaned forward, both hands pressing onto the table's ledge. "More Network members are missing. We have no clue where to find Banks, and if we don't move *now*, more people are going to die." He narrowed his eyes. "But maybe that's what you want. Maybe Marie was right. Is that it, Magnolia? Are you just a plant for your family?"

My power sizzled under my skin. The cabinets rattled, the coffee maker popped. If I broke my new dishes because these two pissed me off…

"That's enough."

I looked at Thirteen on reflex, but he wasn't the one who spoke. Shane gasped. Jon straightened. He looked over my shoulder to the hallway.

Theo towered in the doorframe behind me. His presence wrapped around me like a blanket. I relaxed a little because I couldn't help it. Jon calmed down too, but a new annoyance surfaced in his thoughts. Almost like he did a mental eye roll.

"Theo! Oh, thank God." Shane's hands relaxed at his sides. "We went to your house when you missed the five thirty check-in, and the door was splintered just like Banks's. We thought…well thank God you're all right."

His gaze passed over me and he tensed again—the look on his face even fiercer than before. God, even when I hadn't done anything Shane was pissed off at me.

Theo didn't answer. The tension grew thick but no one's thoughts made sense. What was going on?

"Someone was at your home, Theo," Thirteen said coldly. "Were you there when they arrived?"

Thirteen folded his big arms across his chest. He was concentrating on the break-in scene at Theo's house but…was he *mad* at Theo? That couldn't be right.

"I don't know who took me," Theo said. "I was asleep when they came. The explosion of the door woke me up, but before I could get my gun, I was shot with some kind of tranq. When I came to, I was at the Kelch estate."

"How did you know where you were?" Jon asked.

"I didn't. Not at first."

I felt Theo rotate his shoulders behind me in some sort of stretch.

"You need more rest," I said softly, keeping my eyes on Jon.

"Well, the standoff in the kitchen was kind of hard to ignore."

I almost smiled. Almost.

"But she's right," he continued, "I do need more sleep."

There was a gentle tug on the hem at the back of my shirt. No one else saw, but my whole heart soared. I stepped back toward Theo then suddenly froze in my tracks.

"We need to get through this first," Thirteen said, his words clipped. "Go put some clothes on and walk us through *exactly* what happened last night."

I heard Thirteen, but just barely. Jon had my full attention now: he thought Theo and I had had sex. In fact, he was sure of it.

My mouth fell open. My earlier vision of Theo and me together, only in real life—the thought spun my head. But that wasn't all. According to Jon, finding Theo in a woman's bed was as normal as cereal for breakfast.

Fabulous.

I needed a drink.

For some reason, I couldn't meet Thirteen's eyes. Theo was still pulling his shirt over his head when he reentered the kitchen.

"You sure you don't want to call the whole group together?" he said. "I'm not too keen on telling this story more than once." He pulled out the chair to my left, swung it around, and straddled it. From the way he sat, the blood and tears across the back of his shirt were visible only to me.

"Why don't you just tell us what happened and I'll decide which details are appropriate for the rest of the team."

My eyebrows shot up.

Theo spoke through gritted teeth. "Nothing happened, Thirteen, so how about you back the fuck off."

Thirteen's eyes narrowed. I looked back and forth between them.

After another long minute, Theo said, "Like I said, they tranq'd me with some kind of hallucinogen and took me to the Kelch estate. I assume they dressed me, too, since I was in boxers when I went to bed and in this when I woke." He pulled his tattered shirt from his chest with two fingers. "The drugs had me seeing things that weren't there, so I have no idea which one took me. As soon as they knew I was awake, they strapped me on a table and started slicing up my back."

A need for vengeance washed over me so fast and so strong that the whole room turned crimson. The men, the walls, the light—everything red. I blinked and the room turned back to normal color.

Great…something else that never happened before. What was with me these days?

Theo continued, "After they'd been at it a few minutes, they stopped and one of them started whispering in my ear…in

French. *Qui est l'annuaire?* 'Who is the calendar?' It didn't make sense to me, but there it is."

Wait a minute. What?

"French?" I asked. "Are you sure?"

He looked over his shoulder at me. "Yeah, pretty sure. I only took a couple of years of it in college, but I think I can recognize it when I hear it. Why?"

"It's just that foreign languages—yeah, not my family's forte. The only foreign language any of us are remotely familiar with is Romanian, and that's just because Grandmother lived there when she was younger."

"So you're saying that *none* of your family speaks French?" Theo asked, his voice rising. "So, what? Either I was tortured by someone not in your family, or I hallucinated the question."

I exchanged a frown with Jon then looked over at Shane. He was just as confused. Finally, I turned to Thirteen. His face was ghost white, his expression more void than I had ever seen. And before I could even get a read on his thoughts, he leaped from his seat and raced out of the house.

The rest of us just stared at each other. Then all at once, we jumped to our feet and flew out the door after him. We were just in time to inhale the cloud of dust left behind as Thirteen sped up the gravel driveway.

I went to my car, ready to follow him, when Theo called out, "Mag!" I spun around. All three of them were still on the porch, watching me. What were they waiting for?

"He'll be back," Theo called. The hum of Thirteen's car was fading. We had to hurry. "He's done this before," Theo continued. "He'll come back when he's ready. We just have to wait."

I listened again and the hum was gone. I couldn't even tell which direction he'd driven. *Shit!* I glared at Theo and the others as I stomped back to the house. When I got to the door, I slammed it, leaving the guys on the porch.

I needed a drink. Damn it, something was up with Thirteen and I hadn't caught it. And if Theo was right, all I could do was sit here and wait.

CHAPTER 23

I stayed on the love seat by the front window, ignoring all the others and their patient confidence. All assured and accepting. Their "he's fine" and "he's done this before"—it was wearing on my last nerve. Wasn't *anyone* worried about Thirteen?

No. All they cared about was what information had him acting as he had. They worried about being out of the loop, not whether Thirteen was still alive or not. Bastards.

Theo's image wormed past my mood. Sprawled out over my sheets, his broad chest rising as he slept. I was glad he'd gone back to bed, but the need to join him distracted me. I pushed it away, downed another drink and kept my thoughts strictly on Thirteen.

It was almost nine o'clock that night when Thirteen finally pulled into the drive. Relief washed over me; air filled my lungs once more. The whole team was here now. I pulled my legs up under me. No reason to rush out to meet him. After all, he hadn't even said good-bye. Or called. Or texted.

He ambled through the front door. I nearly choked on my drink. His hair was disheveled, his eyes ringed with dark circles. He looked as if he'd aged ten years in a day. With barely a greeting to anyone, he lumbered into the great room and sat heavily in one of the love seats. His head hung forward to rest in his hands.

"Um, would you like something to drink?" I asked quietly.

He lifted his eyes to mine and smiled. "That would be wonderful, Magnolia. Thank you." I moved to the kitchen in a blur. The next moment I was back at his side, fresh OJ in hand. He took the glass. I took my seat and waited with everyone else. Theo leaned against the wall behind me, a warm weight at my back.

Thirteen finished his drink then clapped his hands together. He took a deep breath and began. "When Theo was in the confines of the Kelch estate, he was asked a single question: '*qui est l'annuaire?*' His translation was correct, but there is another, broader meaning to the term *l'annuaire*. Directory. In this case, the Network directory. *L'annuaire* is the living compilation of our entire membership. Every piece of information about every single member of the Network, present and past, is housed in the well-protected *l'annuaire*…a man named William Broviak."

"William Broviak is *l'annuaire*?" Theo asked after a pause. "A *man* is this directory?"

"That's correct," Thirteen said. He sounded tired, resigned. "You see, William has a special gift, a psychic talent that he has spent the majority of his tormented life trying to alleviate. William sees relationships."

A relationship psychic? Well, let me just add that to my growing list of "what-the-hell-is-going-on."

Thirteen continued, "He has the unique ability to instantly see the connections between individuals the moment he meets someone. For example, in meeting Charles he would know that he is married to Marie, has two brothers in the military; his father, his mother, his coworkers, everyone he knows and has an emotional tie to would be imprinted in William's mind. So when he first met a certain member of the Network…"

"He knew the identity of every Network member," Cordele finished his sentence.

"Exactly."

Hmmm…I glanced back at Theo.

"But none of us knows *all* the members," Charles argued. "We only know those we directly work with. Everyone else is an anonymous face in the crowd. 'You could pass a fellow member on the street and not even know that you both worked for the same elite organization.' Isn't that what you told us from the beginning?"

"*You* don't know every Network member," Thirteen corrected him. "But I do. At least the ones in my division. As a chief in the organization, it's part of my job to recruit and work with every member on their assignments. William was discovered by one of my predecessors nearly twelve years ago. His ability was revealed to the chief at the time and he was put immediately under the care and protection of our agents. And has remained under that protection ever since."

"Wait," Heather said, waving a hand in front of her. "You took him from his life and just kept him? Made him the Network's prisoner just because he had some ability that wasn't his fault?"

She had a point. And I could see where the situation might hit a little too close to home for Heather. Still, she wasn't the only one trying to work through this new information. Everyone's mind was reeling, processing. I took another drink.

"He is no prisoner, Heather," Thirteen said sternly. "He has his own life, however self-destructive it may be." The last he said under his breath. He was getting a headache. And when I saw the man's image in his thoughts, I understood why.

"The smelly old drunk guy at the Turtle?" I announced without thinking. "That's *l'annuaire*?"

"Wait, you mean Bill?" Theo asked from behind me.

"Drunk Bill is *l'annuaire*?" Jon asked at the same moment.

Thirteen sighed so deeply his shoulders fell forward. "Yes, Bill at the Turtle is *l'annuaire*. He's watched by Miller, and others, but refuses to allow us to help him deal with his ability. He prefers to live on the street where people walk past him and look the other way. They just let him be, and he prefers that life to anything we've offered."

So that was Miller's role in the Network—directory babysitting. Thirteen took another drink. *Good idea.* I finished off my whiskey.

"When Theo told us this morning that the only question asked of him was about *l'annuaire*, I had to move quickly to contain William. He was immediately moved to a secure location where he will remain until I assign him keepers and move him to a guarded safe house."

"Do you need this house back?" I offered. *Oh God, please don't make me give up my house already.*

"No. William will be moved out of state." Thirteen shook his head to himself. "We always knew that if the one of our enemies discovered *l'annuaire* it would be devastating to our organization. It's why so few in the Network know of his existence—we couldn't risk someone being broken and leaking his identity."

Shane sat forward. "Plausible deniability."

Thirteen gave one slow nod. I sat forward.

"Then why the hell are you telling us now?" Shane controlled his volume, but just barely. Inside he cursed Thirteen left and right. "Kelches are still abducting Network members—still torturing us for this information. So why even tell us about this guy? Now, if one of us is captured, we'll have exactly what they want."

Thirteen's eyes were cold, his voice controlled. "I tell you because it is now *your* job to protect our most valuable secret. It is now *your* duty to make absolutely certain that our enemies do not acquire *l'annuaire*. The Kelches already know that he exists. We're not going to waste precious time and resources on concealing a secret that has already been revealed."

Marie sat forward, her glare so venomous Jon and Charles adjusted in their seats. "How did the Kelches even find out about *l'annuaire*?" she asked. "None of us knew that he existed. And it's not like anyone here could just pick a word like that out of someone's head. Oh, wait! Yes they could."

What a bitch!

The glass in Marie's hand shattered. "Did you see that?" she gasped. "See what she did?"

"Oh, please," I said and sat back in my seat. "I didn't even draw blood."

"Magnolia!" Thirteen put his arm out as if he were going to hold me back. *I have enough on my plate without having to worry about your temper!*

He was right. Great, now I felt bad. *Sorry.*

He turned back to Marie. "We don't know how the word was introduced to the Kelches. And while other Network members are currently investigating that very subject, *this* team's focus should be on our assignments going forward.

"The Kelches have always had limited interest in the Network. They view us as nothing more than an annoyance or a cleanup crew that sometimes hinders their well-laid plans. They have never seen our organization as a true threat."

I looked at Thirteen. Had I told him that, or was he just that perceptive?

"So why the interest now?" Jon said, finishing Thirteen's thought. "Why make the effort to track down a Network directory if they don't see us as an important adversary?"

"Precisely. Why now? Logic would dictate that either we have done something to cause the brothers more irritation than they have led us to believe, or…"

"Or they really are getting ready to do something big… something that can't afford to be hindered." Shane concluded. He turned to me and glared. God, it was like every day the guy hated me more.

Thirteen looked grave. "Exactly."

CHAPTER 24

The double beep of the alarm sounded. Everyone looked around the room.

Who wasn't here?

"There was an unidentified substance in the remains of the bodies of the Network agents," Thirteen continued, unaffected. "Something that our Network staff recognized only after the initial reports were released. It was so minute in mass that the coroner dismissed the substance as drug residue from the weapons that were used to torture the victims. I had a Network agent analyze a sample of the substance to determine its origin."

The monitor beeped again. The front door opened wide. Everyone in the room, myself included, turned in unison. My jaw dropped. A man, twice the size of the largest guard at the estate—maybe even bigger than Thirteen—appeared in the doorway. He was dark, hooded. Dressed in all black, he kept his shades on and let his shoulder-length dark hair hang forward.

I adjusted in my seat. Unfolded my legs for better maneuverability. Theo shifted behind me. Jon made sure his gun hand was free.

The man was all business. No emotion, no wasted energy on worry or excess. He silently named each individual as he looked around the room. When his eyes found me, his thoughts only stuttered a moment, barely a reaction. And he knew my name instantly. Thirteen must trust this man intrinsically. Not even Banks had been told about me before our personal introduction. So why hadn't I met this guy before?

The man turned his head to Thirteen. From the waistband at his back, he pulled out a sealed packaging envelope. Thirteen crossed the room and took it anxiously. The dark stranger turned to me again. Behind the sunglasses, he met my gaze. My abilities came to him, one after another, as if he were reading them from a list. And he knew every detail—even the new things that I'd never done before now. I moved to the edge of my seat. His thoughts blanked out, gone. A wall had shot up in his mind, blocking me from him. He nodded to me once more and turned away, disappearing out the front door.

What the hell?

I was on my feet. *Who was that guy?* Thirteen shot me the briefest glance as he crossed back to his seat. Slowly, I sat back down. His daughter's image flashed through his mind, his longing stronger than ever. Then he focused again on the package in his hands.

"Who was that?" Cordele asked breathlessly. A pink blush colored her cheeks. She fanned herself with a napkin. I wasn't the only one intrigued by Mr. Big, Dark, and Brooding.

Thirteen tore open the envelope and quickly skimmed the contents.

"Jesse is an old friend," he said finally. His tone made it clear that questions weren't welcome.

Thirteen held up the envelope. "The substance in each of the discovered bodies was polonium 210, a highly toxic radioactive isotope that attacks its victim's DNA. It is exceptionally rare. It is essentially a by-product of uranium. It kills the intended victim by radiation poisoning."

"You mean like victims of a nuclear holocaust?" Cordele asked.

"Not exactly," Thirteen said. "Polonium 210 is only hazardous when ingested. And once in the victim's digestive system, it's death by radiation from the cell level out."

"If the Network members were killed by this radioactive isotope, how could the coroners not pick that up?" Charles asked.

"I don't believe they were killed by the polonium 210. Only miniscule traces of the substance were found in their systems."

"So what does that mean?" Jon wondered aloud.

"As a by-product of uranium, the substance must be generated rather than simply found. And to generate this particular isotope, a nuclear reaction must be created."

Silence filled the room. My stomach sank.

"The Kelches have a nuclear reactor," Theo said, quietly voicing what everyone else had concluded.

"We can't be sure of that," Thirteen said. "But if the Kelches *do* have a weapon of atomic destruction, and a plan to use it, it stands to reason that they would want their chief hindrance eliminated before putting their plans into action."

No one spoke, but their thoughts were all the same: Holy. Shit.

I've asked a great deal of you, Magnolia. I jumped. Then turned dark eyes to Thirteen as his focused thoughts became clear.

More than we agreed to, by far, I snapped.

Yes...I would apologize, but you know in your heart that my intention has never been to deceive or use you.

That's the only reason you're still alive, Thirteen.

He lowered his head and smiled. *I have no doubt.*

So what is it now? I thought.

I don't see another way.

I saw flashes of an unfinished idea flit through his mind. Terror stole my breath. I gripped the sides of my seat to keep from falling over. Heather turned toward me. Theo moved in closer.

You would ask this of me, knowing what could happen?

Thirteen's gaze was frighteningly serious. *They will never hurt you again, Magnolia. I swear this on my life. They will never touch you again.*

Unwanted tears rose at the sincerity of those words. If only he could keep such a promise.

Thirteen's face was tight with wear and intent, his silver hair a little frazzled from the day's stress. His jaw set, his lips pressed. A face I had memorized over the last several months. The face of my freedom.

I closed my eyes. "OK. I'll do it."

CHAPTER 25

Every time I thought of Uncle Max, the same scene came to my mind.

The estate's library. Leaning against an antique desk with his sleeves rolled to the elbows, he fondled one of those pink-gray stress balls.

"Are all the guards really necessary?" he asked.

Father was crouched toward the back of the library using a bucket and towels to scrub my blood from his forearms. "It took eleven of them to get her shackled this time," he groused. "Hell, the bitch ripped off Alec's left arm when he first touched her. And he's loyal even without the drugs!" He grumbled as he wet his towel. "Thank God he's right-handed."

Uncle Max tsked.

I lay on the floor. I couldn't move past the pain in my stomach and lower back. Uncle Max strolled past the four guards posted against the bookshelves, eyeing me as he walked. He played with the stress ball, slipping it back and forth between his fingers, considering my wounds.

"What new ability has she developed?" he asked.

Father shrugged.

"Well she must have developed something," Uncle Max prodded, "or you would have waited until you were in one of the interrogation rooms. You're never in such a hurry that you don't wait to leave the main house. Look at the mess you've made in the study, for Christ's sake."

Father shook his head, scrubbing harder along the backs of his hands. Uncle Max's gaze grew hot on my chest. Bone was exposed, that much I could feel, but it was the blood and muscle that had his attention.

He licked his lips.

I focused on the stress ball in his hands. Looked closer. It wasn't a ball. It was flesh, turned inside out and rolled into a wad. I could smell it now—baby powder over brine. He rolled it in his palms and in between his fingers like some kind of slimy dough.

Whose skin did he play with? I took a focused peek into his mind…and screamed in horror.

...

It hadn't taken long for Thirteen to fine-tune the plan—just a day or two—but it was enough for me to muster up a good amount of dread. We sat in an Econoline van at the rear of the capitol. I was about as spied-out as I could get—dark sunglasses, hair hidden under a Cubs hat, surveillance equipment everywhere.

Uncle Max and my father were both capable of the recent murders. But Uncle Max was the planner. Searching for a Network directory was exactly the kind of big-picture plot he would orchestrate.

Another car backed into its space in the row across from us. Government workers had been coming and going for hours now, but Uncle Max was still a no-show.

Thirteen sighed heavily beside me. "I know you don't want to do this, Magnolia," he said, breaking the long silence between us, "and I don't blame you. But we need to know where to direct our efforts. You only have to get a feel for what the big plan is—why they're so focused on removing the Network now."

He turned in his seat to look at me. A shimmery fog of power brushed along my skin. *Shit.*

"Magnolia…"

One of the monitors in front of us buzzed. Uncle Max had arrived. Bile instantly rose in my throat.

Thirteen pushed some buttons on the monitor, flipped some switches on the dash, and we had sound. Papers shuffling, high heels on tile, fingers tapping on a keyboard—Max's executive assistant readied his office. The click-clack of her heels practically ran from the room. A muffled "Good morning, sir," then heavy footsteps.

My mouth went dry.

Father's mind was cruel, brutal. And Uncle Mallroy's was a frightening void—chaotic, illogical, almost nonhuman. But Uncle Max's mind was sick—like diving into a pool of vomit and dead animals. It was going to take a very long time for me to feel clean after this.

"Fine," I finally said to Thirteen.

I closed my eyes, took a deep breath, and listened. Everything went away—the cars, the people, Thirteen—all that existed was Uncle Max's office. Two interns disagreed in the vestibule. His assistant typed at her desk, fretting whether she had all the information for an upcoming press conference. In the office behind her, Uncle Max sat at his computer, his fingers flying over the keyboard with unnatural speed. His breath was steady, his mind intent.

No. Not his mind. His feelings were intent. His mind was… gone. My pulse sped. I couldn't read a single thought. I focused harder.

"I can't hear him," I said, my voice shaking. "Thirteen, I can't hear him at all!"

What if I'd been gone too long and couldn't read my family's minds anymore? I'd never have forewarning if they came after me. Never be safe. Or what if Uncle Max had gotten stronger? Oh God, what if I had gotten *weaker*? I bolted from the car.

"Magnolia! Stop!"

Thirteen's words came from a distance.

The street moved beneath me in a blur. I was already outside the garage. Lady in blue worried about her children. Man in gray pined for his mistress. The mind of every person I passed came through crystal clear.

I rounded a corner and masked myself, plowing into the capitol invisible. I recalled the layout from Chang's blueprints and raced to the stairs. In a second-floor hallway it hit me, slamming me to a halt. *Uncle Max.*

A wall of power surrounded his thoughts. I couldn't feel it from the garage, but now that I was closer, the power was there like a fortress.

Why would he do that? It wasn't like his enemies could read his thoughts. Only family could do that. And I was dead—or so they thought. Markus and Malcolm weren't strong enough telepaths. Only Uncle Mallroy and my father could really get in his head. But why would he need to protect himself from his own brothers?

I inched forward. The power grew hotter as I approached his office. I could see his assistant's desk from the hallway now.

I took a deep breath, steadied myself against the wall, and tried his mind again. He was irritated. Something from an e-mail. I pushed harder at his mind. Finally his barrier wavered. Another push and I would break through.

I pulled away. My shoulders sagged in a sigh of relief. *Thank God! I was still strong enough.* The air around me thickened. My vision slowly darkened. A light red hue began tinting everything I saw. *What in the hell...?*

Uncle Max shot up from his desk. His heavy footsteps pounded across the floor in my direction. *Holy shit!*

I was back on the street before I had time to think.

So stupid! What the hell was I thinking? Going up to Uncle Max's office—he could have sensed me, realized I was still alive.

My heart pounded in my chest. I wanted to beat myself for taking such a risk. On the stairs of the parking garage I released my invisible mask. My body shook, I struggled to catch my breath. I climbed the steps to the fourth floor. Thirteen saw me immediately.

He stood next to the van, his cell phone to his ear. There was no warmth as he stared down at me. He spat some words into his phone, threw it into the van, and waited, hands on hips.

...

Thirteen's anger was expected. He had yelled and I had taken it, all the while understanding the fear behind his words.

Now that we were back at the farmhouse, however, the others seriously needed to chill out. My stomach already festered at the idea of going back and getting closer to Uncle Max—something I knew I would have to do—and Jon's shouting only made it worse.

"You were reckless, Magnolia! You risked exposure—not only for the Network but for yourself!"

I took a long drink and met Jon's eyes across the kitchen table. "I need proximity to get past Uncle Max's barrier and into his mind. I didn't know that. Now I do."

"You were showboating! We work as a team here. You want to change the plan, fine. But you don't go half-cocked into the middle of the fucking capitol with no backup! Jesus Christ, girl, show some fucking control!"

Instantly, the room pulsed red. Jon's body slammed against the wall behind him. The kitchen's wood-paneled wall buckled in a perfect imprint of his outline. His fingers clawed at his neck. A strangled gurgle escaped his throat.

Thirteen jumped between us with his arms spread wide, trying to decide who to go to first. Theo didn't hesitate. His gun was leveled on me before Jon's chair hit the floor. Shane was quick to race in from the great room but he had to scramble to pull his gun. Heather gasped and her eyes filled with tears.

My eyes were on Jon. Rage simmered inside me. It took everything I had not to rip his head right off. I took another drink. The room slowly dripped back to its normal color. Thirteen stepped forward, but I held up my hand to stop him. Jon remained pinned in place.

"Don't you *dare* talk to me about control," I hissed through clenched teeth. My voice was so low I almost didn't recognize it. Jon squirmed against the wall. Everyone stood frozen.

Then Theo let out his breath. A loud exhale, nothing more. But it was enough. A wave of calm passed over me. With a thud, Jon collapsed to the floor.

Heather scrambled to his side. Theo lowered his gun but Shane held his position. Thirteen glared at me. Whatever. He was already pissed anyway. I threw back the rest of my drink, then poured another.

Theo walked over to Jon and pulled him back to standing. Shane finally lowered his gun. All three turned to face me. Jon coughed a couple of times then found his voice.

"O—OK," he managed. He cleared his throat, rubbed his neck. "Y—you have control. We would all be dead on our feet if you didn't. I get that now." He coughed some more. "Just don't go off on your own like that again. Believe it or not, not *all* of us want to see you killed."

We stared at each other for a moment longer. Then he turned and stumbled his way into the great room, Heather tucked into his side.

Theo didn't move. He just looked at me, eyes dark and wary. It had been reflex to protect Jon. But now...an image of him shooting me played in his mind. Him pulling the trigger, the bullet sinking deep in my chest. I recoiled in my seat, my chest tight with a sudden ache. God, even the thought of being shot by him was painful. But wait—that wasn't *my* pain. I looked at Theo again. His eyes grew wide. His hand moved over his chest. My breath caught.

Thirteen ran his hands over his face. "Come on," he said. "I know we're all on edge, but we need to decide how to move forward." Theo looked at me a moment longer then followed after Thirteen.

I sighed. The red I had seen when my rage boiled over at Jon—it was darker than the reddish hue I'd seen at Uncle Max's office. But in both cases I had felt things I hadn't felt since leaving the estate. Absolute fear, incredible rage—and the dark shade of red had matched perfectly with what I was seeing in my dreams every night.

God, I was so sick of not knowing what was happening inside my own head.

Finally, I rose to join the others. And, this time, I took the whole damn bottle of whiskey with me.

CHAPTER 26

We waited until Friday afternoon. Tempers ran high—people wanted to move faster. But Friday was the only day Uncle Max had no scheduled appointments. He would be in his office all day. It was our best chance.

The van pulled up to the curb at a cross street in front of the capitol. Thirteen had been called to assist in another team's emergency, so Jon drove, Theo in shotgun. Jon threw the car into park, jerking the surveillance equipment piled around me. A line of yellow buses idled across the street. People filled the sidewalk. The buzz of weekend anticipation vibrated through the city.

"You have your panic button?" Theo asked without turning around. I stared at the back of his seat.

"Yeah, I have it." *Think of me. Just once, before I go in there, please think of me.*

Another moment passed in silence.

"We'll be in the garage on Michigan Avenue until rendezvous time," Jon said, also not turning around. "Once you're out of the building, head over to Washington and we'll pick you up on the corner of West and Washington."

Nausea rolled over me but I stamped it down. OK, I could do this. Just stand outside Uncle Max's office, scan his thoughts, and leave. No big deal. He'd sense a supernatural presence again, but it could be any person with powers trying to sneak up on him. He still thought I was dead. Besides, knowing that he would sense my energy gave me motivation to get what I needed and get the hell out of there. Then I could go back to my nice little farmhouse and scrub out my brain for the next few hours.

I looked at Theo again then turned away. With a deep breath, I stretched out my power until I disappeared. Both guys still had their eyes firmly fixed on the windshield. Watching me vanish into thin air was just a little *too* supernatural for even the toughest of tough guys.

Jon jumped in his seat when I slid the van door open. I got out on the sidewalk and looked back into the van. Neither could see me now, but it didn't matter. Theo stared right at me, looked me right in the eyes.

I turned away and closed the door. I dodged cars until I stood in front of the building. My legs were lead as I climbed the white cement steps. Every breath brought another wave of nausea.

I kept to the walls. Last time I was here I'd been too freaked out to look around. The building was beautiful—the domed entry, the statuary and portraits of Americana. I dragged myself to the second floor. The wide marble stairs subtly vibrated. A dull thundering sounded nearby, growing louder.

What the…? *Oh God—Uncle Max already knew I was here.* He must have been waiting for another attempt. Putting out his feelers for another source of power. And he would take out the whole place just to get to me.

I pressed myself flat against the wall. My eyes shut tight. I braced myself. All these innocent people…

Two women strolled by, annoyed. The man at the front desk sighed heavily. A group of men laughed as they walked through the foyer, then mentally groaned. *Field trip day?* What the hell was field trip day?

As soon as I thought it, the stairs overflowed in a stampede of children. Hundreds of them. They poured down the steps in a waterfall of activity and chatter. Thank God I was against the wall, or they would have just plowed right over me.

I waited for the wave to pass. The poor adults followed in their wake. They looked more like zombies than chaperones. I smiled to myself. Max *hadn't* sensed me. I could still do this.

Renewed confidence had me flying up the stairs. I'd bent his barrier earlier—I could take it out today. But when I reached the vestibule outside Max's office, my confidence stumbled. His power was everywhere. Thicker than before. Instead of a fog that I could wade through, the power actually pulsed around me. Alive, active. Evil.

He'd sensed me the last time, all right. And he had upped his protective wall as a result.

A few deep breaths and I forced myself to move silently into position. I chose a corner of the vestibule beside the two leather chairs that faced Uncle Max's assistant's desk. It was three o'clock and she was closing up shop to get a jump on the weekend. She worried about picking up her kids on time, what she was fixing for dinner, if she could get a date for tomorrow when the kids were with their dad. Normal, everyday thoughts. Nothing at all about my family.

How often did Uncle Max screw with her memory to keep her so oblivious?

She shoved some files into her briefcase, pressed some buttons on her phone, shut down her PC, and rose from her seat. My heart stopped in my chest. Would she open the door to Max's office, to say good-bye? It was bad enough being this close to him. If I had to actually *see* him again…on reflex, I gripped the little panic button clutched in my hand.

But once her desk was in order, she simply strolled out into the hallway. My whole body relaxed when she was gone.

I looked at the closed door. *OK, you can do this.* I closed my eyes, took a deep breath, and centered myself. The weight of his power breathed against my skin. His barrier was like cement around his thoughts. Rough, solid. I had barely brushed up against it when something pulled my concentration away.

Warmth spread though me, settling the knot in my stomach. A few blocks away, Theo was thinking of me. After days of being intentionally preoccupied, he finally let down his guard. He felt helpless, angry, like it should be him standing outside Uncle Max's office instead of me. Thirteen should never have put me at risk like this. Never.

My body tingled. The lingering panic inside me calmed. A soothing confidence took its place. I might have Kelch blood pulsing through me, but I could still help the people around me. And today…I would do exactly that.

I pushed off from the wall and stood just to the side of Uncle Max's door. He was at his desk again, fingers flying at the keyboard. I took another deep breath, closed my eyes, and pushed.

Whoa. That was one powerful wall. I pushed out a little harder. The typing stopped.

My heart pounded. *Now or never.* I concentrated my power until my body shook. The wall in his mind shimmered, turning from cement to Jell-O. I was in. My gag reflex went into overdrive—the sheer sadism, the uninhibited evil. Blood, pain, joy, all mixed in together. The barrier tightened, tried to solidify once more. My power wouldn't let it. Then suddenly…the barrier pushed back.

My own mental walls slammed into place. His power scraped over my skin and mind. Thick, like an icy syrup. Cold enough to bite. I shivered. His power pulled back.

I let out a shaky breath. *See, you can do this.*

The next instant, I was off my feet, flying backward into the wall behind me. My muscles spasmed in pain as my head exploded. I slid down the wall and landed in a heap on the floor. I tried to catch my breath but the pain kept coming. Excruciating. I ground my teeth together to stop from crying out. The pulsing power surrounding Uncle Max's office had turned to twisting pierces everywhere it touched me. My flesh, my mind. Red hues tinted the room as my consciousness started to slip.

There was a wailing. Like a siren inside my head. Blaring, echoing all around me. The floor trembled beneath me. Passing out meant dropping my invisible mask. I *had* to stay conscious.

But there was so much pain. And I'd been away too long.

There was movement. My eyes couldn't focus. The wailing got louder. I felt Uncle Max's presence as he entered the room. *Oh my God—he's right there!* My body violently cramped as another surge of power lashed out through the room.

Just stay conscious. Just stay conscious.

He was right in front of me. I shut my eyes tight. The pain fought to pull me under. I was going to lose it.

From some great distance I heard Uncle Max's terrifying voice call out over the blare, "Not yet! Not yet! *Who the hell is in here?*"

For a horrific instant I saw his mind clearly. Then all went black.

CHAPTER 27

Just as pain had pulled me under, pain brought me back. A dull pressure softly pulsed at the back of my head. Annoying at first, like a headache after the Tylenol wore off. But it quickly sharpened, became piercing. Before I knew it, my entire head was swallowed by fierce, painful throbs—a direct hit to my mental powers. I couldn't even tell if I was invisible anymore. My telepathy swirled out of control.

Oh God, please don't let this happen!

There were at least two people in the room with me, maybe more. Fear, confusion, anger—every foreign thought bored into my mind like metal spikes. I tried to breathe, to settle my muscles. I *had* to regain control. Warm tears leaked from my eyes.

On the edge of my mind I saw it. An escape. Empty and gray, a cloud of nothingness crept on the fringes of my thoughts. So dull in its appearance, yet so brilliant in its appeal.

This was the madness that had taken root in Uncle Mallroy's mind—the emptiness that I feared more than anything.

God, no. It had appeared in my mind only once before. The memory of it sent me into tremors. I had thought I could conquer the madness, use it as a temporary escape when my family was being especially cruel.

I had been wrong.

The madness was *too* empty, like turning off reality and personal control altogether. Giving in would be losing myself as well as my consciousness. Defending myself would be impossible. I'd be completely unaware of how my powers were used. I couldn't let it take me or I might never find a way back.

My tears turned to sobs. The gray fog pressed further, deeper into my mind. Fear slowly overwhelmed the pain. But even worse than the fear was knowing that somewhere deep inside me, where I would never admit it out loud, there was a piece of me that had always *wanted* the madness to take over. Insanity would be a freedom—an excuse not to care about my family or their evil or the consequences of my powers.

There was movement around me. My body tensed as another shot of someone else's worry drilled into my mind. A comforting burn touched my lips. I swallowed instinctively and the burn slid down my throat. I gulped it again and again until there was nothing left. The gray fog slipped away.

Aah. So much better. I took several deep breaths and just savored the feel of my own control. Slowly I pried open my eyes. The images blurred together. I blinked the room into focus. Thirteen stared down at me. His eyes were bloodshot and his face pale. His voice was raw as he whispered, "Magnolia? Can you hear me?"

I lay on my bed at the farmhouse. The sheerness of my yellow curtains made the evening light glow more white than gold, brightening the room more than it would have otherwise. Thirteen had pulled a chair from the kitchen to sit beside my bed. His face was tight.

Where was Theo?

I started trembling. Couldn't breathe, terrified of what had happened to him.

Thirteen sat straighter, scooted his chair closer. That's when I saw him. Leaning with his back against the doorframe. A bottle of whisky dangled from his hand. My tremors calmed instantly. *Theo. Still beautiful. Still perfect.* The ache in my chest rejoiced. Any lingering pain flew right out of me.

"Are you OK?" he asked. He spoke as if we were the only two people in the room. Maybe in the world.

"Yeah," I said softly, "I'm good." He stepped toward the bed and my body automatically shifted toward him.

A strange noise escaped Thirteen, freezing me in place. *Oh, right, Thirteen's still here.* His head hung forward, his eyes closed.

"Thirteen?"

His huge shoulders lifted in a trembling sigh. "I thought you were dead again," he said in a strangled voice. "I prayed you'd come back, that you'd heal like before, but you didn't even have a pulse. Not at first." He shuddered and covered his face.

"I tried to stay conscious, stay invisible. But Uncle Max's power was blaring—it was everywhere. And then he came into the room. He came over to where I was knocked backward and..." My heart raced again. Sweat beaded on my forehead. My fingers curled into the sheet. I should have been too spent to muster real panic. But the thought of Uncle Max looming over me, his face contorted in such a familiar rage—it was too terrifying. Thirteen drew a ragged breath. Theo reached out and touched my ankle under the sheet. Instantly my fists relaxed.

"How did you get to me?" I finally managed.

"Your panic button set off the Homeland Security alarms," Thirteen said after clearing his throat. "That was the blaring you heard. Security was immediately sent in to retrieve all the congressional officers. There was a stampede of government employees exiting the building. Jon and Theo were able to slip in after the security guards pulled Maxwell from the room. You were still invisible when they found you."

Still invisible? So passing out *hadn't* revealed my cover. Then what *had* made me visible again?

"I found you," Theo said quietly, as if reading my thoughts.

"How? If I was still invisible?" God, my voice was scratchy.

"I just...*knew*. I knew where you were."

He stood beside the bed now, his hand still resting on my ankle. Instinctively my hand lifted. My fingertips itched to feel the solidness of his arms, his face, his body. Thirteen shifted beside me. I blinked and dropped my hand.

My mouth opened and closed a few times but my throat was too dry now to make words. I wanted more details, but for once I thought I needed something other than whisky.

"Your camouflage dissipated when Theo, well, when he touched you," Thirteen said, eyeing me closely. I looked back at Theo. For once he didn't look confused or like he was searching for some explanation. He looked possessive. A raw hunger darkened his eyes. My insides somersaulted at the look. Not because it worried me or had me questioning again our growing bond. But because it felt right. He should be possessive. I belonged to him.

I shook my head and forced myself to focus. "I—I didn't push the panic button," I said.

"When Jon and Theo found you, the key fob was so deep in your palm the button was still being pressed." Thirteen relaxed a little then and reached out to touch my forearm. "Magnolia, what happened?"

I closed my eyes for a minute. "Uncle Max sensed I was there and sent out a mental shock wave."

Thirteen's eyes went wide. All the color left his face. "He sensed you?"

"He sensed *a supernatural presence*," I corrected myself quickly. "He didn't know it was me."

My throat was in flames now. But before I could ask for a drink, Theo was there, a full glass of water in his hand. His fingers brushed with mine as I took the glass, and I gasped. *Oh God.* It was just like in the kitchen all those weeks ago—that brushed contact so much more than a firm touch. I could see it so clearly I stopped breathing. Theo, holding me, his calloused hands running up and down my arms as I pressed into his bare chest. My body sliding perfectly into place along the length of his. "Mag…" his lips had moved against my cheek as he breathed into my ear.

"Mag?" he said again, louder this time. I opened my eyes. Theo now sat at the foot of the bed, his hand moving slowly up my calf. He leaned toward me, his breathing as heavy as mine. That possessive look was more than just a dark gleam in his eye now. His shoulders were set, his jaw flexed. His lips parted.

"Ahem," Thirteen cleared his throat. A shiver swept up my spine, bringing me back and reddening my cheeks. Theo blinked rapidly, shifting his body away from me. But his hand remained on my leg, the contact still there.

"The important question is," Thirteen said, shooting pointed glances at each of us, "why did Maxwell leave with the security guards? Why didn't he just mind-manipulate the guards so he could stay behind and find out who was in his office?"

I took a long sip of water. *Just stay focused.* But his hand was so warm. So strong against my leg. I closed my eyes tight.

"If security was making all the senators leave the building, there would have been questions," I said quickly. "People would have reported his absence and, as powerful as Uncle Max is, he can't keep track of every single person in the building at one time. And if the media were there, it would have already been on TV that he was still inside. He and Father rely too much on their public images to risk something like that."

I gulped more water then shrugged. "Or, hell, maybe he was just so thrown by the idea of someone actually trying to break into his thoughts that it didn't even occur to him to mess with security's minds."

Theo's fingers traced circles on my calf. "Yeah, I can see how you'd throw someone off like that," he murmured, his voice rough. *Oh. My. God.* To just be alone right now, curled up beside Theo. The trace of his fingers—I felt it everywhere. So much more than just a touch sliding along my leg.

From the doorway behind Theo, Jon stepped into the room. I jumped. How long had he been there? I hadn't even noticed his arrival. *Shit.* That wasn't good. I should have felt his presence in the house. When he glanced my way, accusations were all over his face.

"We still have some questions," Jon announced. Theo frowned and pulled his hand from me. His thoughts were jumbled again. He got to his feet and stepped away from the bed as Jon walked into the room.

"We still don't know what Senator Kelch's intentions are against the Network. We need—"

"Yes, we do," I interrupted before Jon's rant could really get going. "Uncle Max has no intentions."

Jon and Theo both gaped. "What?"

"I *saw* into his head, just before everything went black. Policies and politics, and even some very not-nice things that might be happening soon." I turned to Thirteen. "The Network needs to up its protection on Senator Claussen, but we can talk about that later." I turned back to Jon. "But there was nothing, absolutely nothing, about the Network. Nothing about recent tortures or atomic weapons; nothing about *l'annuaire*. Nothing. Maxwell isn't behind the attacks. He doesn't even know about them."

I sank completely into the pillows. The hit that my mind and soul had taken in the last several hours was catching up with me. Then to have Theo pull away like that—I closed my eyes and moved the sheet a little farther up my body.

"Well," Thirteen said finally. "That's going to change some things."

My eyes stayed shut but I felt the bed move when Jon leaned over and pressed his hands down at the foot of the mattress.

"Are you sure?" he asked. "Because that just doesn't make any sense. We all agreed that an attack against the Network would have to come from the brothers, most likely with Maxwell at the helm. If he's not behind this, then who? Do we go after Magnus? It has to be one of them."

I shook my head. God, I was so tired. "No. It doesn't work like that. If Uncle Max doesn't know anything, then neither do the others. They can't keep secrets from each other. Their minds are too closely linked."

At least it had never worked like that in the past. But Uncle Max was blocking his thoughts now. *Why?* I was too tired to explain this new development and they wouldn't understand anyway.

Jon didn't like my answer. "What do you mean it doesn't work like that? Doesn't work like what?"

Exhaustion tugged at my consciousness. The pillows were so cool and soft.

"Magnolia, what do you mean..." Jon started again.

"Jon," Thirteen's voice was low and soothing and commanding all at the same time. "We can discuss it further in a few hours.

For the time being, it's been a long day and we all need some rest. We have enough information to begin rethinking our next steps. Let's just leave her be for now."

Thirteen's big hand patted my forearm. His warmth felt good, safe. He wouldn't pull away from me just because other team members were around. I heard the shuffle of feet and felt a dip in the bed as everyone moved to leave. I cracked open an eye.

Theo still stood in the doorway, and that new look of possession was back. I shivered under the weight of that look. He stared down at me for another moment before he finally turned away. Softly, he closed the door behind him.

I fell back against the pillows. I hadn't even realized that I'd leaned toward him.

CHAPTER 28

In my dream, there was only red now—crimson and salty—full of power and rage and rightness. In this dream I knew myself. I knew my likes and dislikes, my strengths and weaknesses—every nuance of the emotions and power within me. There was no more confusion, no more doubt. I pulsed with the certainty that I was everything I was meant to be. Complete in every way. And I totally welcomed it.

The crimson deepened and expanded, soaking into my skin like a sponge and turning my flesh a deeper, purplish pink.

Utter bliss.

My body relaxed as my powers swelled. My muscles flexed and my bones shifted. But there was no pain. I was being molded. And that was just fine.

A flash of light burst from my chest, but the crimson thickened, began to coagulate. On reflex, I pulled against it, but its solid grip tightened. Quiet uncertainty stirred. The crimson was acting on its own, struggling against my pull, and I struggled to wake myself, but the dream itself did the same, resisting me.

Another golden flash.

My chest clenched tighter than ever, and I gasped as a clarity approached my consciousness. All those flashes of color I'd seen while awake—it wasn't part of the dream at all. It was a part of *me*. It was the fear and the rage and the pain, welling up and taking me over.

Thirteen's face appeared before me. What was this? There had never been people in my dreams before. I lifted a hand to wave him over but the red held me tight. Then he turned to me. His hands clasped the sides of his head, his eyes poured red, adding to the sea of red around me. Blood. And I was reveling in it.

I pulled again, this time with force. It still wouldn't give. Theo appeared then. *Oh God.* And Heather. They reached for me, red spilling from their fingers, their throats, their mouths. The rightness and fulfillment I'd felt earlier vanished, shut off like a light. The red magnified, nearly purple now. My flesh blackened as the blood continued to fill me from the outside in.

Another flash of light shot out. *I* was still here, still in control. I gathered strength from every piece of energy I had left. I would *not* hurt them. I would *not* let the red take me. With one final pull I wrenched myself free.

I awoke, gasping, my body shaking violently. My heart pounded in my chest. Evil pulsed deep inside me. And if I let it, it would carry me away.

I put a hand to my head just to make sure it was still attached and felt that I was soaked in sweat. The backs of Theo's fingers brushed along my neck. I jumped with a yelp. He crouched beside the bed, frowning at my panic. The vision from my dreams pierced my mind—his pain, his blood. All from somewhere inside me. I shut my eyes tight. When I opened them, he was still there, frowning harder.

Theo's sun-kissed hair framed his face. His eyes looked even deeper and more beautiful than usual. Slowly, his presence calmed my racing pulse. I could breathe deeply now.

I leaned back against the pillows. He reached out again, his hand moving with me as I lay back down. His fingers gently traced a path along my jawline. The movement was so natural, he didn't even realize he was doing it.

"Everyone's gone," he said quietly. "You want to hear about the next plan of action?"

I shook my head *no* before he even stopped talking.

I didn't want to think about what was coming or who we were targeting next. I didn't want to know the Network's next plan to use me for my powers. I didn't want to think about the blood in my dream or how wonderful and right it felt to soak myself in it. He kicked off his shoes at the foot of the bed. Then he looked back at me with a new hesitation in his eyes.

I took him in, his perfect tan and his tight T-shirt that emphasized the definition of his chest. I sat up and pulled the sheet back on the side closest to him. Then I relaxed back into the pillows and watched the smoothness of his muscles flex and ripple as he slid under the sheet next to me. His clothes were still on and he had yet to touch me, but my entire body grew warm and tensed in places I didn't know could tense. But when he reached out and touched my chin again, this time lifting my face to meet his eyes, my body released itself.

He held my face with the touch of his fingers. I closed my eyes and turned my head into his palm, gently forcing his entire hand to cup my cheek.

"Magnolia…" he breathed. My body flexed as a steady pulse built inside me. My powers swelled beneath my skin. Theo's hands moved from my face to pull me to his chest. I rested my head on his bicep as his other arm wrapped around me.

"Sleep, my Mag," he whispered. I let him hold me tighter and let the confusion of the unknown wash away. I drifted into a serene sleep.

This time, I dreamed of gold.

CHAPTER 29

"You know, your attitude really sucks."

The next morning when the others arrived for the briefing, Shane decided to take it upon himself to fill in the role of asshole now that Marie was away with Charles and Heather on *l'annuaire* guard duty.

"I'm just trying to understand what the hell happened yesterday," he snapped at me. "The whole 'I would have seen Magnus's thoughts in Maxwell's head' thing—it's bullshit! It doesn't make sense!"

I took a long pull on my whiskey and slammed the glass hard on the table.

"I don't know how else to explain it other than exactly the way I have already explained it like a hundred times!"

There was something else tainting his thoughts. An anger that had nothing to do with the mission. I'd felt it the moment he arrived, but his thoughts were racing and pulled in all directions.

I couldn't tell what his anger was about. Maybe he'd had messed up dreams last night too.

Whatever it was, Shane reeled with questions. And the order for more investigative research had him pissed to an unreasonable level. He didn't trust my detail of the events and felt we shouldn't steer away from Uncle Max just because I *claimed* he wasn't behind the Network abductions.

"Shane, man, we've been over this," Jon said from the counter, where he finished off the coffee. "We need to completely change our approach. Thirteen's decision is made. So either offer something new, or shut the hell up."

Cordele sighed from the seat next to me. She spun her glass of OJ on the table between her hands the same way I spun my whiskey. When had she started doing that?

"We'll just see when Thirteen gets here," Shane mumbled under his breath.

I rolled my eyes. "Where *is* Thirteen?" I asked.

Jon and Theo exchanged a quick glance, then frowned. Immediately, both men whipped out their cell phones and punched speed dials.

"Nothing on his cell," Theo said after several moments on the phone.

"No answer at home," Jon replied at almost the same time. We looked at each other, the same thought in mind, and were on our feet, moving toward the door without a word. Jon was in front but I was tight on his heels. He stopped so abruptly I stumbled into his back. "Where do you think you're going?" It took me a moment to realize he was talking to me.

"Where the hell do you think I'm going?" I said.

Jon opened his mouth, an order for me to stay already on his tongue. My power flared. *Just try it, Polo Boy.*

Theo put a hand on my shoulder. His fingers brushed against my neck. Warm comfort trickled through me as I slowly turned to face him. His eyes softened the way Thirteen's did sometimes—patient. "Thirteen would want you to stay here," he said quietly.

I narrowed my eyes but couldn't hold it. Against my will, I calmed down.

"If he's not OK, or if we need your help, we'll call," Theo continued. "I promise."

And just like that, I knew I wasn't going anywhere. *Damn him.* Using our connection to manipulate me like this. If I could, I'd be totally pissed off at him. As it was, respect grew inside me. Smart guy to recognize a valuable resource when he had it. *Crap.*

He held my gaze a moment longer then walked out the front door.

Cordele turned to me as she backed down the front hall. "Do you have our cell numbers in case you hear from him?"

"Yeah, I got 'em," I said and snatched up my whiskey bottle.

"We'll be back soon," Cordele called. The screen door bounced on its frame behind her.

I poured a tall glass of whiskey, no ice or sour mix. Might as well finish off the bottle. Not like I had anything else to do.

...

I stretched out on the extended sofa in the great room. I'd never tried this before, but what the hell? Everything else with me was so out of whack, this might actually work. I closed my eyes and concentrated. *Where are you, Thirteen?* I focused on his image—the little crinkles around his eyes when he smiled. The deep tremor of his voice. His comfortable scent of Old Spice and ginseng.

Nothing. After a few minutes more I gave up. I couldn't sense him.

I took a long drink. Thirteen was a tough guy. He'd been fighting my family for years. He was probably just working through something with one of the other teams. I mean, he came back last time, right?

But the others weren't worried last time. This time they were.

The gore from Uncle Max's thoughts flashed in my mind. Blood coated his every thought. Pulsing inside him, just like my dream. Did he draw strength from that darkness? Did his powers swell inside him every time he made someone bleed?

Uncle Max had said that their powers grew as more vessels carried our bloodline. Torturing his victims wouldn't grow his powers, would it? When I lashed out at Jon, throwing him against the kitchen wall like that, everything had turned red—just like when I was near Uncle Max. The rage and fear had come easily, naturally. Had I gotten more powerful in those moments? I couldn't be sure.

In my dream I'd recognized the source of the supernatural pulse inside me. My powers fed from that place; in my dream, whenever I'd resisted the red, gold light flashed. The same color gold I dreamt of lying beside Theo last night.

So what the hell did that mean?

...

Markus hid in the cover of the tall shrubs that surrounded the estate's southern gardens, watching as our father and uncles stood in a semicircle before Grandmother. Each man wore a pressed suit—tailored and expensive, just the way Grandmother liked.

Her long silver hair and flowing red dress blew in the breeze. She would have been beautiful, radiant even, but her face was contorted with so much rage that her features looked sharp and frightening.

She hissed words that had no meaning.

Suddenly, Uncle Max's face turned menacing. Inhuman. His posture hunched, his hands fisted. He launched himself at Father, tackling him to the ground. Power sizzled in the air. Rocks from the garden path levitated and the breeze gained strength, swirling debris all around them and shaking the bushes where Markus hid.

He wanted to run, but was too terrified. He couldn't move.

Father and Uncle Max grabbed at one another, tearing, strangling each other with their strength. Then, as if he had to join the fray, Uncle Mallroy grabbed Uncle Max by the throat and flung him across the garden, smashing his body into a tree some fifty yards away.

Father's eyes were liquid fire. He crouched—more animal than man—and leaped at Uncle Mallroy, taking him down with a roar. It was like watching wild dogs attack one another, unable to stop even if they wanted to.

Uncle Max returned, sending a mental shock wave into the other two, but both were on guard and returned the fire and attacked again as mindlessly as before. Blood coated all of them, suits shredded.

Grandmother's hair whipped around her face. Her eyes burned with excitement. A smile stretched her lips. Then she turned to the bushes where Markus hid, and she laughed.

...

It wasn't my memory. I'd seen it in Markus's mind when I was a child. I'd been surprised he'd had the guts to spy on them, but glad he did because it gave me the most detailed memory I'd seen of Grandmother.

Kelch had been her surname, not Grandfather's, and she had epitomized what it meant to carry the legacy. Callous, manipulative, bloodthirsty. Evil. She hadn't needed supernatural abilities to control her powerful sons. And power was all that ever mattered. Economic power, political power, supernatural power—it didn't matter. She wanted it all, and through her sons, she got it.

Soaking in the blood of my dream, feeling the rage and fear pulse around me, it had felt soothing, right. Just like I imagined it would have felt right for Grandmother. But something was changing inside me—new feelings, new powers. And those felt right too. My knees curled up to my chest and I buried my head in my arms.

The night before, Theo had wrapped his arms around me. Comforting as my confusion washed away. God, how I wanted to feel that again. Even more, I wanted to be someone who Theo *should* want like that. I wanted to not be a Kelch.

Enough of this. I wiped off my face and finished off my drink. Then I went to the kitchen for a refill. I was what I was. No amount of want or self-loathing would change that.

The double beep of the alarm sounded. Soon after, I heard footsteps on the porch. Heat flared inside me. My hand froze halfway to my mouth. He was back.

CHAPTER 30

Theo pulled open the door and walked through the kitchen. I'd returned to the great room and had to fight the urge to leap off the couch and go to him. I clutched my drink like an anchor.

He glanced around. "Where is everybody?"

"No one else is back."

He pulled out his phone from his back pocket. With a shake of his head he scrolled through missed messages.

"Any word on Thirteen?" I asked.

He kept his eyes on his phone. "I haven't gotten through to him, but I think Jon's got him tracked down. We're waiting for Cordele to report in."

I sat back on the couch in relief. After another moment I asked, "You, er, want a drink or something?"

"I can get it," he said quickly. He slid his phone back in place and spun into the kitchen. I leaned in to watch as he found my whiskey bottle amid the mess on top of the fridge. He took a long draw straight from the bottle. A drop escaped his mouth, trailing a stream of liquid down his jaw and onto his neck. I licked my lips. That whiskey must taste incredible against the salty stubble on his throat.

He grabbed a juice glass and the open bottle then ambled his way into the great room. He paused in the molded frame that separated one room from another. We both took another drink.

"So," he said as he moved cautiously to the other end of the couch. "Any luck figuring out what's happening with all the, er, supernatural stuff?"

God, he smelled good.

"I don't know," I fumbled. "There's a lot to figure out."

He nodded to himself and stared at his glass. I had a sudden urge to twirl my hair. *Why was this so awkward?* It hadn't been awkward last night when he'd cradled me to his chest. Run his fingers through my hair; pulled the covers over us both. I ran my eyes over his face and saw, where his shirt gaped at the collar, the dark ink of a tattoo.

"What is that?" I pointed to his neck. "That right there, what is that?"

Startled, Theo looked down at himself. He pulled the collar back to reveal the tip of an elaborate tattoo. "This?" he asked. The black ink had faded to a dark green on his skin. "It's a tattoo. I got it years ago."

I gave him a look. "I *know* it's a tattoo. But what's it *of*?"

He frowned again, hesitated. "It's a coat of arms," he said finally. "It's my family's coat of arms."

"I thought you didn't like your family," I said, my voice quiet. I remembered the vision of his mother. Then the story of her family.

"I don't," he said. "I hate them, actually. That's why I got the tat—as a reminder of who they are and who I will never be."

My head flipped up. My mind spun with excitement.

Whisky and hesitancy forgotten, I crawled across the couch on hands and knees. When I was so close that the next deep breath would have me in his lap, I rose up on my knees. And smiled. His thoughts wavered. I lifted the hem of my tank top to just above the dimple of my belly button. His breath hitched. Steeling my courage, I undid the top button of my jean shorts and pulled down the front of my already low-riding pants.

"Look," I said eagerly.

He didn't respond. I looked at him closely. His eyes were glazed over. His thoughts fuzzy. After a moment, he blinked himself into focus. Ran a hand over his face. Finally, he forced his eyes to follow my gaze, down my body to where my stomach melded into my hip bone.

"The ink is raised," he said in a husky voice. "Wh-what is it?" He continued to blink rapidly. His thoughts became more alert as he took in the tattoo's intricate design.

"It's the Kelch family crest," I told him. "My brothers gave it to me on my fifteenth birthday. They found me chained to a table after one of Father's sessions and thought they'd try torturing me themselves. But it didn't hurt. Not at all."

Theo reached out and brushed his fingertips along the rough imprint on my skin. This time, *my* breathing hitched. His touch was so gentle, so warm. I doubted I would ever get used to such rough hands caressing me instead of punishing me.

Theo looked up into my eyes. My face heated. I was suddenly nervous in a way I'd never been before. I couldn't even tell what he was thinking. Or what would happen next.

Theo's calloused fingers no longer caressed my hip, but clung to it. His other hand reached to my face. He brushed the hair gently behind my ear, cupped my cheek, and stroked my temple with his thumb. His eyelids dropped a little. My breath turned to a pant, and my hands slid along the firmness of his chest. I grasped his shoulders. My legs moved on their own, lifting me, one leg swinging over his lap. The movement brought my opened jeans even farther down, forcing the palm of his hand around to my lower back.

His fingers on my face trailed lightly down my cheek, brushing along my jawline. My lips parted and I pressed into his chest. His other hand curled beneath the waist of my jeans. Still not close enough. Our faces moved together. Our noses brushed and my vision blurred. Finally, our lips met.

His mouth was soft, a contrast to the steel muscles coiled under the rest of his skin. He was controlled, unhurried, gently opening my mouth to brush his tongue against mine. I'd never felt anything like it. His fingers were suddenly up, tracing every line, every curve of my face. Reassuring me as his tongue continued to taste my mouth in a rhythm that even someone as inexperienced as I was could recognize. My eyes slid shut.

He adjusted beneath me, just enough to make all the difference. He slid down on the couch, one hand twisted in my hair, the other firm on my hip. Gently he moved me against him. The bulge in his pants rubbed perfectly against my core. In a gasp, my shirt was gone. Panic lit up inside me, but his soft eyes kept me in the moment. No judgment, no anger. He clutched me tighter against him. His hands kneaded at my back. His warm breath was ragged as his lips moved from my mouth to my chin then down my neck.

A new heat stirred low in my body. An exciting pressure, simmering. Fear of what was happening struggled against the desire to never stop. Theo guided our rhythm, fueled the heat inside me until I was on the brink of boiling over. *Oh God, what was happening?*

And then suddenly…everything changed.

The room glowed. Our skin shone with a golden light. My breath pulled out of me as if on a string. I exhaled without end until there was no more breath to release. When I breathed in, it wasn't air I drew into my lungs, but gold. I watched it trail into my mouth in a gentle and vital inhale.

This golden bond solidified between us.

All barriers, all reservations, disappeared. His heart beat in time with mine. I could feel my touch on his skin, feathers of electricity brushing along his shoulders. The softness of my hair against his palm. The sensations as real and solid as his firm weight beneath me. My mental walls evaporated. His thoughts came flooding in.

Perfect. More. Oh, God what is she doing? What is happening to me? So beautiful, so broken. No. No. No! Don't be a dumb-ass! Stop yourself!! So much power. Too much power. She's the one that's a supernatural, not me. I have to stop. Stop before it's too late! Oh, she feels so good, so perfect. We are perfect! God I have to stop this. She's a fucking Kelch, *for chrissake!*

My heart stopped as the gold faded and air whooshed back into my lungs.

Chapter 31

Air expanded in my chest. Theo gasped. He shivered from the sudden absence of power between us. Eyes wide, he studied my face. And just as I'd expected, he paled in fear.

"No," he breathed. "I didn't mean it like that."

The walls in my mind slammed shut. I didn't want to hear any more. My eyes closed too, but the tears came anyway. His sorrow and guilt and fear left him speechless. I turned away.

I was a Kelch. That's all that mattered. Our closeness hurt now.

The front door flew open. We both jumped.

I'd been so wrapped up in Theo that I hadn't even heard the beeps of the alarms. *Damn it!* Jon, Shane, and Chang sprinted into the house. Before I could think, Theo grabbed a throw blanket from the arm of the couch and threw it over my shoulders. He wasn't quick enough.

My bare back, my jean shorts lowered as I straddled Theo's lap—Chang fell like a board, face-first, slamming onto the great room floor.

"Oh, great," I mumbled. *Could this moment get any more humiliating?*

Jon gaped—shock plain on his face. Shane's expression was hard. Was he *still* pissed off?

Then it hit me. Of course he was still pissed. I was a Kelch. God, it was so obvious now. The sidelong glances, the constant edginess, the subtle shifts away from wherever I happened to be—it may not have been forefront in their thoughts but it was perfectly clear now. I would never truly be accepted by these people. Somewhere in the backs of their minds, I would always be the enemy.

"No!" Theo's eyes locked on my face. "You are not the enemy."

Had he just…? No, that was impossible. Theo wasn't telepathic.

Jon coughed loudly, shuffling his feet. "We, er, have some news that can't wait," he said.

"Of, of course," I stammered. My cheeks burned as Jon tried unsuccessfully to avert his gaze. "Just…just give me a minute."

I slid to the side, peeling myself from Theo's lap. His hands grabbed tightly onto my upper thighs, holding me in place. His eyes bored into mine—angry, determined, and something else I didn't recognize. My eyes burned as I held back the tears. I pulled away from his grip and clutched the blanket to my chest.

My body felt odd, more solid as I moved. The connection between us was stronger now. Like a palpable weight inside me. I might be a Kelch, but that didn't change the fact that we were more linked than ever before. The reality left me feeling very… breakable.

I gripped the blanket tighter, quickly gathered my discarded shirt and bra—*When had my bra come off?*—and raced to my room.

He waited to waylay me in the kitchen when I came back but I didn't give him the chance. I was refocused on my job and responsibility—I had to put him aside for now.

I swung around the long table and plopped down on the faded ottoman in front of Jon. Theo stood at my back, his presence more discernible than ever. I could hear his soft breathing, feel his pulse, feel the heat inside him as his frustration grew.

Yeah, no distractions there.

"So what's up?" I asked Jon, totally businesslike.

After a quick glance over my head, Jon went into a long explanation about a text message he'd received from Thirteen. I tried to pay attention. I *wanted* to pay attention. But my insides ached as if ripped apart.

"Did you hear what I said?" Jon said loudly, probably for the second time. *Ugh! Stupid, distracting...*

I quickly read his thoughts and gasped. "*Ohmygod!*" I jumped to my feet.

"Right," Jon said. "So any suggestions on what to do now?"

"I have to go get him."

"Whoa, whoa, whoa!" Jon was on his feet in front of me. Shane and Theo jumped up as well. "We don't even know where he is."

"Of course we do. Theo was held at the estate. Thirteen must be there too."

I moved to sidestep Jon. He cut me off. The room's atmosphere suddenly shifted. Aggression seeped into the air all around us. My instincts took over. I adjusted my position. My power itched beneath my skin. Jon held his position in front of me, blocking me from the door. His hand moved to the butt of his gun.

"You said that your father and uncle weren't the ones orchestrating these attacks. What makes you so sure they're being held at the estate?" Jon's voice was deep, deliberate.

All my senses were on alert. I chose my words carefully. "Like I said, Theo was held at the estate. I don't know who is behind the attacks, but it makes sense that the others are being held where Theo was."

"And yet you didn't see the need to return to the estate until now. Until Thirteen." His voice was so low it came out in a hiss. "Was this your plan, Magnolia? Set up Thirteen's capture then return to your family?"

"Oh, for Christ's sake!" My stance relaxed. I rolled my eyes. I should have known this was where his thoughts were going. *Stupid distractions! I was missing everything!* I pierced Jon with a look. He took a step back.

"Listen to me very closely, Jon," I said, my voice like ice. "Thirteen is the one and only person in my entire existence to truly care for me." Theo shifted behind me. "I will do whatever it takes to get him away from my family. Whatever it takes."

I let the threat hang in the air as Jon processed my meaning. His hand fell away from his gun. "Whether he's being held there or not, it's not like we can just walk onto the Kelch estate and start looking around. It's something the Network has tried in the past with exceptionally bad results."

"But *I* can go," I insisted. "I can search the grounds undetected." My stomach dropped at the idea, but I held my ground. Jon looked at Theo.

"What about getting in his head and bringing him back the way you did me," Theo said tightly. "You can get him out of there and not have to risk yourself."

"I already tried that. It doesn't work on him." I glanced at Theo over my shoulder. When I turned back to Jon, concern softened his glare. He was truly torn.

"Jon," I said, keeping my words and tone as civil as possible. "I will not lose Thirteen. And *you* are not capable of retrieving him."

I could see his next argument coming.

"I do not report to you, Jon, and I sure as hell don't take orders from you. I will find Thirteen and I will bring him back." I stalked into the entryway and laced up my shoes.

"You can't do this by yourself," Theo called out. His long strides brought him quickly through the kitchen and into the hall. I fumbled with my sneakers. The laces caught in my fingers. Why couldn't I tie my freaking shoes?

Theo and Jon exchanged a look and once again their thoughts mirrored one another. I glared up at both of them, ready for an argument. A loud scrambling from the great room stopped us all. *Great. Now what?*

Chang moaned from the great room floor. I rolled my eyes again. Shane went to check on him.

"Too much, dude," Chang moaned. "That chick is just too much."

"Don't worry," Shane said, and shot me a glare of pure venom. "Apparently she's suicidal. We won't have to deal with her much longer anyway."

"What the hell is your problem?!" The room shimmered. My vision darkened as red tint shaded everything around me. I stifled a gasp. *Shit!* It was so close to the surface now. A little agitation at Shane and—bam!—my blood dream came to life. I forced some deep breaths. Once my vision was normal again, I turned back to Shane. "What in the world did I *ever* do to you?"

"You exist!" he snarled.

That was it. Thirteen's abduction, Theo's hurtful thoughts, my powers acting up—I'd had enough. And Shane's perpetual attitude was just the outlet I needed. I narrowed my focus and drilled into his mind in the most violent way possible. *Mindsweep.*

His hands flew from Chang's arms, dropping the man back to the floor with a thud. His fingers pressed hard to his temples. He crashed to his knees with an ear-piercing cry. Guilt tightened my chest but I didn't stop. At least not until I saw the buried reason behind his anger.

Shane cared for me. Really, *really* cared for me. So much so, he didn't know how to handle it. The images in his mind were like a slideshow of every moment I'd ever been near him. When I'd first entered the conference room of the Thirsty Turtle. Sitting beside him on the way to Banks's house. The first time I'd smiled in his direction. And every magical illusion I'd created in training. He had found inexplicable joy in everything I had done.

And he hated himself for that.

My family had killed his parents. He'd hated me before he even met me. But when I walked into the conference room that first time, everything changed. He saw the bond forming between me and his teammate—a teammate with a long history of getting whatever female he wanted. Nothing would ever happen between Shane and me. He hoped that knowledge would be enough. It wasn't. He didn't want to care for me. He simply couldn't help it.

"I'm so sorry," I whispered.

He met my eyes. Tears streamed down his cheeks. Because I had been so cruel, he knew what I had seen in his thoughts. I couldn't speak for what I'd done.

"Shane? You all right, man?" Jon had pulled his gun and was pointing it at the floor in front of me. Shane lowered his head and wiped a hand over his face.

"I'm good," he said finally. He pulled himself to standing and brushed off his clothes.

"Is everything cool here?" Jon asked, his eyes darting between me and Shane.

"Yeah, it's cool," Shane said. He ran his hand from the back of his neck over his hair and down his face. Then he shook his head like a wet dog. "So what's the plan?"

I just stared at him. What could I possibly say?

"Take the blueprints," Chang called from the floor. "They're still in my car."

Shane once again bent down to help. Theo moved behind me. He lifted his hand, reaching for the side of my arm. I moved swiftly out of his reach. Shane's pain was too close to my own. And now wasn't the time to deal.

"I'm going after Thirteen," I said to Jon, needing to get back to business. "But his retrieval will be my only concern. If Banks or anyone else is there, I can't guarantee their safe return."

Jon measured me for a moment. He gripped his gun tighter but left it at his side.

"So any other captives are the Network's responsibility," Theo said from behind me.

I kept my eyes on Jon. He cocked a brow. "Is this your way of asking for backup, Magnolia?"

"This is my way of telling you where my loyalties lie." My voice was cold again. "If you come onto the estate with me, I can get you in undetected, but my only concern will be Thirteen. I won't have your back in a fight with my family, and you cannot defeat them on your own."

"You aren't the only one who cares about Thirteen."

"But I *am* the only one who can get him back."

The room hung in the pregnant pause. Shane finally spoke up. "We're coming with you, and we'll bring *everyone* back—including each other. So let's get organized."

Jon nodded in agreement. So did Theo.

"Fine," I snapped. "But get organized in the car. We've got to move."

We marched out the door to Jon's Cherokee. The metal screen bounced against the frame behind us.

"I'll just be here on point," I heard Chang call out as we hit the driveway.

Good. At least someone would live to tell the others what happened.

CHAPTER 32

According to the clock, it was early afternoon, but the sky was thick and black. Thunder growled on the horizon. The temperature had dropped about ten degrees in the last forty-five minutes. I wanted to blame my growing nausea on nerves from the pending storm. But it was the perfectly landscaped lawns that really made me cringe. Everything was so *perfect* on the north side. No overgrown cornfields, no little run-down farmhouses, just golf courses or stringently maintained community parks. No one on the north side ordered carryout from King's Rib like we did during training.

After maneuvering several trail-lined side streets, I directed Jon to pull over at the wooded edge of the property's far east side. Jon turned the Jeep onto a dirt inlay behind a thick grouping of trees and parked out of sight.

Chang had provided property lines and structural blueprints of the estate. Jon, Shane, and Theo huddled in the car, outlining their rescue plans for any other hostages found. The dry wind twisted my hair, and scents of the southern gardens wafted through the air. I was really here…returning to the place where nightmares came true. Thirteen *had* to be my focus. It was the only way I could continue breathing.

"We can hike it from here," I told them.

Each man adjusted his weapons as we exited the car. To survive here, I had to rely on instinct alone. No feelings, no thoughts…just survival. With a deep breath, my mind relaxed into a state of suspended animation. Power hummed beneath my skin. I was all senses and strength now, pure instinct. I shuddered at the familiarity of the feeling, at the necessity.

"Mag."

Warm breath whispered at my neck. Theo's heart-wrenching thoughts tripped through my mind, but the force of our connection still calmed me. My breathing steadied. I kept my back to Theo as he placed his warm hand at the base of my neck. My powers surged. Golden light tinted my vision. Just a touch from Theo now and my powers jumped to this new level. Hell, this was even more intense than the red.

His hands lingered, fueling the power along with the urge to get closer to him. Another moment and I stepped away, shrugging him off. It was all just too raw. I turned away from him but I held tight to the swell of our bond inside me. At least something good came from this mess with him—my control was reinforced steel now. My thoughts, my instincts, my powers—everything that made me *me*—kicked into gear with evolved focus.

Voices began to come through. Four captives, over a mile away—never before would I have been able to hear their thoughts so clearly. Now I could pinpoint their exact location, hear their individual minds.

My lips stretched into a wide grin. "Here's what we're going to do."

We stood in a close circle behind the Jeep. The best way to enter the estate would be over the southern wall. I used Chang's blueprints to outline where the cameras were and the distance from the camera view to a "safe" area inside the grounds. We would go over the wall as a group so I could camouflage our appearance as we moved. Once in a safe area, I'd pull back the camouflage so they could each see where the others were.

"Thirteen and three other Network members are being held in an old two-story horse barn on the southeast acreage. Two of the members are awake, but injured. The third is unconscious." I kept my tone distant, focused. "Thirteen is in the gated room on the second-floor loft," I continued. "The others are downstairs in the former storage rooms. There are seven men guarding them who—"

"Wait a second," Jon interrupted. "How the hell do you know all this? Are you sure about the other hostages, because right now just Sasser, Thirteen, and Banks are expected to be—"

"I can hear them," I said impatiently.

"You sure you didn't know all this ahead of time?" Shane asked through clenched teeth.

My hands fisted. The world flashed red, but only for an instant. My control was resolute. "We are *here*. We are about to go over that fucking wall. If you people don't believe in me by now then just *go the fuck home*. I'll do this myself!"

Jon stepped between us, his arms outstretched as if to hold us back. I bit my tongue at the irony: wasn't it Thirteen who had jumped between *Jon* and me, in that very same position, just a couple of days ago?

"That's enough!" Jon yelled. Theo had his gun gripped in both hands, but pointed it at the ground in front of him. "We cannot get over that wall and to our captured teammates without Magnolia's help, Shane. So either get on board with the plan or return to HQ with Chang." Then he turned to me. "Magnolia…hell, we may never completely trust you. That's just the way it is, so get over it. But right now, for this mission, we have no choice but to get your back. And we *will* trust you to get Thirteen out of there safe and alive."

He looked back and forth between us. "Now everyone calm the fuck down and get your game faces on. We've got work to do. Magnolia, you said there are seven guards in the barn. Any of them your relatives?"

"One is, but I can't make out who it is. Whoever he is, he's strong. I can get inside his head, but I'd rather wait until we're over the wall." *When the temptation to haul ass out of here will be less distracting.*

"Will he sense you," Jon asked, "like the senator did back in his office?"

"Once I get close enough to the barn, yes. He'll be able to sense a supernatural presence, but he won't know it's me."

Worry flashed through Theo's mind, but it was gone just as fast.

"You're not going to see me once we reach the barn," I continued. "I'll be invisible and will stay that way until I have Thirteen. You three worry about the other captives."

"Once we have the members," Theo said, "we'll head south back toward the wall."

Jon added, "We'll rendezvous back here. If we need backup, Chang will be ready to make the call." He stood straighter, a new gleam in his eye. "Things go well, and the Kelch family will have a better appreciation for the abilities of the Network."

I rolled my eyes. "Let's just do what we can to get Thirteen and the others and try not to get killed in the process. OK?"

We each exchanged glances. All three cocked their guns. And we were off.

Chapter 33

All three guys were solid masculine specimens of training and muscle. Still, they were no match for my speed and strength. I had to practically walk for them to keep pace. Who knew working with a team would be so *frustrating*. And even worse was their noise. Did they *try* to step on every twig on the freaking planet?

You're just irritated to be back here. Stay focused.

We approached the wall. I stopped several feet inside the tree line. I wanted the cameras to be on the out-turn, just to be safe. When the lens began its rotation away from our position, I stretched out my power and concealed all four of us.

They were quicker than I expected. We were over the wall and safe inside the opposite tree line in under a minute. I pulled back our invisible cover. They looked ready, capable. I put a finger to my lips and listened. No security breach had been detected. We moved again, quicker this time.

A few minutes later we neared a clearing and I pulled up short. I listened again. There was no time to take in individual thoughts, but from what I could tell, all four hostages were still alive. At least for now.

Nausea stirred in my gut. One of my relatives was in that barn. I could feel him. But which one? And where were the others? Steeling my resolve, I took a deep breath and scanned the rest of the estate. Father's study was empty. So was his master suite. The library, the interrogation rooms, the dining halls—all empty. I reached out farther, focusing just on the remembered sensation of Father's energy. Across the gardens, into every building on the estate, there was nothing.

Relief washed over me, nearly buckling my knees. *Thank God!* My father wasn't home. I hadn't realized how worried I'd been about facing him again. But now, knowing he wouldn't be a factor, I was practically giddy. I lifted my face to the sky. Rain had started to drizzle but I didn't care. Anything was possible now.

I listened again. Uncle Max was at his desk in the main house. He talked on the phone—an overseas call with someone in Africa. I could hear the translation device speaking in that pleasant robotic voice.

My father and Uncle Max are occupied. That means it's either Markus or Malcolm with the hostages.

I spoke to all three of my teammates' minds simultaneously. One of them flinched. I didn't care. My father wasn't here. Uncle Max wasn't in that barn. Taking out one of my brothers would be nothing. In fact, I didn't even bother finding out which brother it was. I just started moving again.

"What about Mallroy?" Jon whispered. This time *I* flinched. How could I have never noticed how loud these people were?

Mallroy is a nonfactor.

"But—" Jon started again. A severe glare cast over my shoulder cut off his words. Uncle Mallroy wasn't an organizer. They knew that. He rarely ever took part in his brothers' plans. It would be a wasted effort to focus on him now.

The barn is on the other side of the clearing up ahead. The north side door will be closest to the back storage rooms where the hostages are being held. I can mask your appearance to the guards until you are in position. I'll be upstairs getting Thirteen.

I paused a moment and looked at each of them. All their training, all my preparation. They were still no match for my family's powers. Not even my brothers'.

I'm going to mask my appearance early. Be ready for a fight. A hard one. And please—please remember what I showed you about the illusions. My brothers' powers aren't as strong as Father's or Uncle Max's, so if you're ready for them, they shouldn't be a problem.

From beside me Theo lifted his hand, reaching out as if to touch my arm. Instantly I vanished. All three of them sucked in a breath.

"Let's go." I said.

...

I guided them with my thoughts. We crossed the clearing to the broad side of the barn. The last time I had been here, I'd eavesdropped on my father and uncles. Everything looked the same, except that the maintenance crew had replaced the wide swinging doors with an automatic garage door.

One guard—Allen the Asshole—stood at the front of the barn, so we moved against the wall to the opposite end. The camera that monitored the north door, a regular wooden door, had been disconnected; its cut wires dangled from the top of the doorframe. Had my brother done that?

No one will be able to see you, but it's good to know that the monitor is out of commission.

"Wait," Shane whispered.

Shhh! I yelled in their minds. *Just think it and I'll hear it. If you want me to tell everyone I'll relay it, but you've got to shut up!*

Fine, Shane thought at me. *Should we wait for you and Thirteen to cross the wall or just meet you back at the Jeep?*

I turned and looked at Shane. His features were tight. He couldn't see me but he was turned in the right direction to face me. God, he really did care about me.

Thirteen won't be invisible, I told them. *Once you're in place I'll pull back my power. Everyone will be able to see you. I'll keep Thirteen safe. As soon you see him, follow his lead. This way the Network will be the responsible rescue party. Secure itself as a viable threat to the family. Once you're over the wall you are outside of Kelch property lines. You can take the hostages to the police, or a safe house, or whatever you guys do with Network witnesses.*

We've never had witnesses before, Jon responded. *Not against the Kelches. No one's ever survived a Kelch capture before. God, if we can save the witnesses, we could really take out the family. Destroy them. The Network lawyers could…*

Whatever! I said. *Let's just stay on track here.*

Thunder crashed in the distance. A good storm would mask our escape. A great storm would knock out the power. I'd just keep my fingers crossed.

OK, I told them, *this is it. On the other side of the door is a tall partition that leads to the left and ends at the storage rooms. The rooms are small, like closets. There are three guards posted outside. I can keep you invisible until I find Thirteen upstairs. Get in place as quickly as possible and be ready for your cover to drop. The stairs are just to the right of the door. That's where you need to watch for Thirteen. Are you guys ready?*

All three thought *Ready* at the same time.

My powers heightened in anticipation. Each man vanished before my eyes. We were all invisible again. I turned back to the barn and went to the door.

Theo was at my back; I could sense it. I welcomed the calm his nearness provided right now. My powers shimmered, anxious to use this new level of energy inside me. *Here we go.*

With a deep breath, I pulled on the door's long metal handle. It opened easily. I moved quickly along the inside wall, leaving room for the others to enter behind me. The guards at the end of the hall jumped to attention. To them the bolted door must have seemed haunted—opening and closing all on its own.

"Who's there?" a tall guard called out. He stood in a ready fight stance, his hand moving for his gun. The two behind him mirrored the move. They wore solid-colored wife-beaters and baggy jeans as if they were a uniform. Like wannabe gangsters with white trash roots. Father must be hurting to find decent guards if he'd lowered himself to hire these guys.

"Sir? Is that you?" the same guard called out.

Whoa—what? These new guys knew the family's supernatural secret? How? Most staff had to be employed for at least a year before being exposed to the Kelch "otherness." Something wasn't right here. Someone brushed against me. Theo, Jon, and Shane made their way down the partitioned hall. I took a step to follow them, then stopped.

No. This was their fight, not mine. They could handle themselves.

I turned my thoughts back to Thirteen and sprinted the short distance to the rusted staircase. All the bolts were so rusted out that it barely hung from its joints on the second floor. I flew up the stair on tiptoes, hoping not to collapse the whole thing.

The narrow second-story loft stretched the length of the barn. The ceiling angled with the roof and had more cobwebs than secure nails. Slowly, I inched over the plywood floor. The stall-turned-room was at the far end.

Thirteen's thoughts were weak but alive. His guard's thoughts made me frown. Something about that guard…

A stroke of my brother's energy hit me from across the barn. I froze midstep. My stomach dropped. *Markus.* His voice echoed through the rafters from the barn below.

"…big one will give," he said to a guard. "We just need to find the right pressure point."

My confidence wavered. The pain, the hatred—he wasn't as bad as my father, not by a long shot, but he was still part of my life here. I closed my eyes and focused. His voice was barely recognizable. I knew it was him, felt it in my bones. But he sounded deeper, scratchy. Like he had a sore throat.

That was weird. None of us ever *got sick.*

Whatever. It didn't matter. All that mattered was that he was downstairs. Not in the room ahead of me. I crept through the loft toward the open doorway. An enormous masculine shadow passed by the doorway. A clang quickly followed.

"We both know that you'll give up *l'annuaire* eventually," the guard growled. "Might as well make it easy on yourself."

My heart leaped into my throat. I recognized that guard now. *Shit.*

CHAPTER 34

"Do you have any idea what will happen to you, Thirteen?" Banks asked. His gravelly voice paralyzed me where I stood. "It will be unbearable. You get that, don't you? You *will* be broken. And the directory will be taken anyway."

A loud metal pounding shook the cobwebs from the rafters. Banks passed the doorframe once more. "Damn it, man! Do you think I *want* to watch you suffer?"

Thunder clapped. The barn brightened in front of me, pulsing red with every step I took. I didn't even try to push it back. I could see Banks through the doorway. My hands shook as I inched closer. There was a burn inside me now, and it was spreading fast. I ignored the hot ache and continued forward. Still invisible, I slipped into the small room.

My heart stopped as agony ripped through me. Banks stood hunched over Thirteen, his hands wet with the blood of his former boss and mentor. The red hue of my vision vanished. There was only dark crimson now. True rage.

I stood opposite the door, taking in both men's profiles. Banks, in all his distortion, leaned far over, nose to nose with Thirteen's swollen face. Blood from Thirteen's wounds coated his body and pooled on the ground at his feet. I wouldn't have even recognized him if not for the weak voice of his consciousness.

The burn in my stomach ignited. Like electricity on a wire, my body sizzled with power. A sharp current whipped through the room. Thirteen's eyes slammed shut. His head shot back against the chair holding him. Banks fell to his knees with a clang. His hands clutched the sides of his head. Both men screamed.

Holy shit! Instantly, I reined in my power. The burn inside me simmered, anxious to strike out again. And all around me the crimson pulsed. Ready, sure, like some sort of high. So…fulfilling. Right. My blood dream come to life.

Thirteen's eyes popped open. He turned his head as best he could against his restraints, looking around the room. He knew I was here. As weak and shredded as he appeared, he was still Thirteen. And he had a plan. I stood back and waited. Ready for his signal.

Banks was on all fours in front of Thirteen's chair. He panted, adjusted his leg.

"He's getting impatient," Banks snarled at Thirteen. "Either you tell me what I need to know…or you tell *him*." He jerked his thumb over his shoulder, pointing to the open barn below.

As if Markus could send a violent burst of energy through the barn like that. *So fucking stupid.*

Thirteen shifted in his seat. He was in so much pain. I wanted to run across the room and heal him right now. *Just wait one more minute. Let Thirteen do his thing.*

Thirteen's mouth opened but no words came out. Finally he managed to whisper, "Why?"

Banks looked up from where he knelt on the floor and then threw back his head in deep belly-aching laughter.

"As if I'm going to have a heart-to-heart with *you*!" He barked another laugh.

But Thirteen wasn't asking for himself—he was asking for *me*. And whether the piece of shit Frankenstein monster planned on confessing his motives or not, I heard. Money and power. So simple, so petty. A beautiful townhouse full of priceless artwork, cash flow without end, a false promise of supernatural power. Even someone as loyal as Banks could be swayed to the dark side.

The burn inside me swelled again. I'd enjoy killing Banks for his betrayal. No, not just kill. Mutilate. Tear him apart until he begged for mercy. But my control was solid. Consciously, I elevated the burn within me. Power expanded beneath my skin. I trembled at the feel. *Amazing.* This wasn't me defending against one of my father's attacks. This was me using my power how it was *supposed* to be used. As a weapon.

With pinpoint precision, an intense wave of concentrated energy shot from deep inside me, piercing Banks in the temples. I shuddered in a wave of pure, unadulterated pleasure.

The big man staggered. His enormous hands clutched the sides of his head as a terrible cry ripped from his throat. I could feel the pain inside him, and it fueled my burn. The more agony I created within him, the more my power gained strength. How could I have ever questioned this violent feeding of my powers? I could feel the blood inside him, coursing and heating up. It pulsed faster and faster, louder and louder, until the crimson of the room pulsed in time with Banks's anguish. *Delicious.*

"Urgh!" Banks bellowed. His fists pounded against his head in panic. The clangor of his heavy leg shook the rafters as he scrambled to his feet. He started for the door.

I was faster.

Banks slammed into me like a brick wall. With a crash, he rebounded onto the floor. I laughed as he landed hard on his ass. *So fucking pathetic.*

Slowly, I pulled back my invisible mask. Time he learned what it *really* meant to work with a Kelch.

CHAPTER 35

Banks froze at the sight of me standing in the doorframe. His mouth opened and closed but the crashing thunder drowned out his pitiful mutterings. I sauntered over to where he'd fallen to the floor. His eye widened and I hesitated. There was something in his look I'd never seen before. The rough Network enforcer I knew was gone. In his place was a man overcome not with fear or horror, but complete adoration.

"I never told about you," he whispered, his voice articulating the worship in his eyes. "I never told him you were alive. Never even thought about you. I swear it."

It was the truth. His thoughts were too raw to lie. Apparently, Shane wasn't the only one more taken with me than I had realized.

I crouched down in front of him. With gentle fingers I caressed the puckered flesh around the stitching of his eye patch. I leaned in close. My face brushed against his hair, nuzzling his cheek. His heart skipped. His breath caught in his throat. And I felt the rush of his blood traveling to his groin.

"If it was to *me* that you kept allegiance," I whispered, "then your loyalty has been seriously misdirected."

I refocused my power, this time specifically into my hands. I'd never done anything like this, but it felt so natural it was easy. Growing and stretching against Banks's mottled face, my hands curved into something I'd never seen before. The bones and muscles cracked and shifted, realigned into larger, fiercer talons.

I smiled. The power flowed through my hands and completed their change. Then, with the silky force of knives, my fingers curled into his skin and ripped the eye patch from his skull.

Banks's mouth opened to scream. Again, I was faster. With a quick squeeze of my other claw, I crushed his vocal cords. Only a gurgle escaped. I dropped the eye patch to the floor before my long, sharp nails returned to his face. Slowly, I scraped along the gaping wound of his lost eye.

"You really think my family would ever share anything of value with someone as pitiful as you?"

A small sound came from Thirteen's direction, but I couldn't make myself turn away. My nails gently moved across Banks's forehead, leaving trails of bloody lines over his brows. His body convulsed in violent shudders. Tears streamed from his eye. The blood that flowed from his wounds spilled out and coated my strange and contorted hands. I could almost taste its tangy bitterness.

In fact, before I realized what I was doing, I leaned over. My mouth moved toward Banks's wounds. A strangled noise bubbled in his throat. I cradled his head in my long hands. My lips parted instinctively.

"Magnolia."

I froze, my lips moments away from tasting his flowing blood. Thirteen's voice stopped me. "Magnolia, don't."

I blinked. The dark red of my vision dimmed, a semblance of normality returned. Banks's head rested between my inhuman hands, but it was like I was seeing him for the first time. *Oh my God.* What had I just done?

With arms trembling, I let him go. He fell to the floor in a heap. Slowly I backed away. All I could do was stare. The blood pooling around him, the desecrated flesh on his face—all evidence of the torture I had just inflicted. Proof that I was just like everyone else in my family. But worst of all, the torture had felt so right. It still felt right. *This* was what it meant to be a Kelch.

"Magnolia…"

In the next moment I was in front of Thirteen. Instantly, his restraints fell away. He swayed in his chair then crumpled forward. I held him up, my clawed hands on his shoulders. I used my forearm to wipe the blood from his face. The wound would be on the very top of his head. I searched through his hair, eager to heal him.

"Thirteen? Thirteen, can you hear me?"

Finally, I found a deep gash at the top of his forehead, right along his hairline. A perforated blade had been dragged along his scalp. It ran nearly ear to ear. *Damn those bastards!* Banks convulsed on the floor behind me.

I placed my elongated palm on the top of Thirteen's head. My energy flowed through him. It worked much faster than it had with Theo, or even Charles. My powers were stronger now. Within seconds he was completely healed. His sigh of relief filled me. But when he opened his eyes, there was a question in his look.

"What is it? What do you need?"

"Stop torturing him, Magnolia." His voice was real now, commanding. No more struggled whispers.

Banks twitched on the floor, curled in the fetal position. I put an arm around Thirteen's shoulders and helped him up. We walked together across the room, where I leaned him against the doorframe. I stepped toward Banks. Thirteen grabbed my shoulder. "He has suffered enough, Magnolia."

"I know," I said, not looking at him. "I'm ending it."

But as I approached Banks, the burn inside me returned. Red colored the room again. This time, though, I pushed it away. I was *not* like my father and uncles. I would not give in to this. I crouched on the floor beside Banks. His one eye pried open. So much terror in his gaze now. Images of all the things I could do to him raced through my mind. The pain I could cause him—such a sweet temptation. *No. I won't do it. I won't.*

Banks's eye shifted to the doorframe. The moment he glanced away, I clutched his heavy head between my clawed hands and twisted. His neck snapped. A shiver swept along my spine. I closed my eyes and shuddered. It was done. I placed his body gently on the floor.

I didn't look into Thirteen's face. Not even when I wrapped my arm around his waist and started across the loft for the stairs. Something told me I really didn't want to see his expression right now.

CHAPTER 36

Gunshots and violent cries echoed through the barn. The guards on site had reacted quickly when the others were revealed. At the top of the stairs, I listened to find out how many more were on their way, but no alarms sounded in the distance. Markus had disarmed all the barn's monitors. *Why would he do that?* The thunderstorm raged outside. We were nearly a mile from the main grounds, and no one else at the estate had noticed us. At least not yet.

I stretched out my power until Thirteen and I were invisible. We headed down from the loft. Thirteen gained strength with each step, but I still forced him to the inside of the stairs. Halfway down, the stairs whined in protest. I hoisted Thirteen and raced us to the floor. Behind the partition, the three hostages were seated on the floor, propped up in front of the door. One had Jon's extra gun, another swayed in his fight to stay conscious, and between them both was a lump. Hair and clothes bloody, the unconscious third hostage.

A fight was underway across the barn. Six men still battled. One of them was Markus. The rest were dead. A part of me ached to confirm our men among the living, but I refused to listen. I needed to get Thirteen away from this place. Now. If I let myself think for even a second that something had happened to Theo…

I shook my head. We were at the back door. I could hear the rain pelting outside. I tightened my grip on Thirteen. *Time to get the hell out of Dodge.*

"Magnolia, stop," Thirteen ordered. "Release our cover."

I shifted us behind the partition and pulled back my power until we were visible. "What?" I snapped. We *so* did not have time for a powwow right now.

The hostages gasped. Thirteen stepped in front of me, blocking me from the door.

"What are you doing?" he asked.

"I'm getting you out of here," I said. "Hopefully without any of my family realizing I still exist."

I reached around him to open the door. The handle slipped from my grip. Banks's blood coated my fingers—normal fingers now. I hadn't even felt them shift back. Thirteen moved in front of me again. His legs shook under his weight. Bullets bounced around the room. Several cut into the partition in front of us. We needed to get out of here. Now.

The intensity of Thirteen's frown made me pause. Blood seeped into the creases of his skin. The endearing crinkles were now hard and frightening lines.

"I will not leave my men, Magnolia," he said. "If you wish to save yourself from exposure, no one will stop you. But I will not leave without all my people with me."

My chest clenched. He wasn't really choosing the others over me. But it sure as hell felt that way.

"But I came for *you*! To get you out of here. I can't leave you here."

His gaze softened. "Then stay. And help me fight."

One of the hostages shifted, his body bruised and broken. Thirteen knelt at his side.

"But I'm just another Kelch to them," I whispered. A sob choked in my throat. A bullet embedded itself in the wall next to my head. The two conscious hostages gasped. I didn't move. Slowly Thirteen rose and rested his hands on my shoulders.

"I promised you that your family would never hurt you again. But I can't protect you from the hurt you may receive from others. You need to decide how many of these new experiences you can handle. But for right now," he dropped his hands and stepped back, "I have a fight to join."

He turned and vanished around the partition.

"*Motherfuckinggoddamnpieceofshit!*"

The cries and blasts of the fight drowned out my tantrum. The two hostages looked up at me with wide, swollen eyes. The one with Jon's gun adjusted his grip. Now what was I supposed to do?

I rubbed both hands over my face. *Fuck!* Finally, I took a deep breath and listened. Theo and Shane were still on their feet, fighting the one remaining guard. Relief flooded me, but only for a moment. Then I focused again. All the other guards were dead. Jon engaged Markus at the far end of the barn. And damn it all, Thirteen had just joined Jon in his fight.

Fucking idiots! What part of just-grab-the-hostages-and-run-like-hell didn't they understand?

Markus fought with his telekinesis and his strength. But he wasn't at full power. I couldn't make out why. Was he wounded?

That didn't make sense. His maniacal laugh cut through the room, taunting his two opponents. If he were injured, he would simply kill the humans responsible then skulk away to nurse his wounds.

"Fine!" I yelled at the two men at my feet. They both jumped again.

God, just let Thirteen survive.

CHAPTER 37

I turned the corner of the partition and froze.

Along the far wall, Theo and Shane had used up their ammo. They fought a massive, drug-controlled guard with knives. All three men were bloody and worn. The guard's head was shaved bald; his muscles bulged. I didn't recognize him, but he fought well, obviously experienced.

Shane crouched to pounce at the man's back. He leaped into the air, his knife ready to kill. But midflight he turned, faced the other direction, and slashed at empty air, fighting another opponent who wasn't really there—an illusion. Theo took on the guard alone.

Near the barn's garage door, Jon gripped a two-by-four with both hands. Blood poured from a gunshot wound in his shoulder. But his fight remained fierce. Unfortunately, he too had been distracted by something that wasn't really there. And Thirteen was moving in to help him.

A demented bark of laughter rang out. Markus stood on top of a tarp-covered heap, his eyes wild. My heart stopped.

Markus, my handsome and fearful brother, was now a hideous skeleton of his former self. His skin was tight over bones and lean muscles. A deep purple scar cut diagonally across his face. The puckered flesh left a cleft in his lips and sliced one eye in half, the white, milky eyeball on full display. His thick waves of dark hair were cut short, buzzed above the ear to show grated flesh. The rough flesh spread down the side of his neck and under his shirt collar.

My God, what happened to him?

Shane screamed and fell on his back, still holding off his imaginary assailant.

OK, enough of this.

I stepped into the openness of the barn. Instantly Markus's illusions vanished. Jon and Shane both stumbled. Theo spun on the guard's back, slicing the giant's throat with a swing of his blade. The guard's bald head fell back, gleaming brightly as a flash of lightning illuminated the room.

Markus frowned, his scars pulling taut.

"Markus!" I called out.

He spotted me from across the room. Astonishment, confusion, disbelief—Markus's mind was total chaos. Good. Let him stay confused until I got the others to safety.

"You're dead," he said, matter-of-factly. "We checked. Several times, for days, we checked."

"Yeah, guess it takes a little longer to heal a beheading." I moved forward cautiously.

Slowly, his thoughts became more defined. Angrier. I could feel his powers gaining strength. Markus narrowed his eyes on me, and the intensity stopped me in my tracks. A tinkling sounded to my left. A rumble to my right. Suddenly, every piece of farm equipment and the tools scattered around the barn launched at me at breakneck speed. Someone shouted my name.

The tools and instruments halted midair. With a clamor, they fell to the ground several feet away from me. I cocked an eyebrow.

"Seriously?" I asked. *Had his scars left him stupid as well as ugly?* "What happened to you, Markus?"

"What happened to me?" he asked; his power chilled the room. Thunder crashed outside. *"What happened to me?"*

"Yes, Markus," I said dully, "what happened to you?"

"What do you *think* happened to me?" he shouted. Spittle flew from his mouth. "The Kelch power must be harnessed. They needed to strengthen their energies, practice their skills." His good eye dilated to blackness. "I told them it was me! I told them *I* was the one who killed you, but they didn't believe me. They believed *Malcolm*."

His anger peaked at the mention of our other brother.

"*He* was the one they accepted. *He* was the one they let stay in the main house. I was left with nothing. Nothing! Cast aside to be nothing more than their plaything."

His body shook. He opened and closed his mouth. Sounds escaped but no words formed.

"You took my place," I said finally. "For their frustrations and their experiments—but you can't heal yourself, can you, Markus? You couldn't take it the way I could."

"You fucking bitch!" he screamed. Boards, nails, dropped weapons all flew at me again. Again they fell short by several feet. "Why couldn't you just stay dead like the other one?"

I paused. *What?* "What the hell are you talking about? What other one?"

"The other one! The one they killed when they should have killed you."

Markus vibrated with rage. His thoughts slowly became clear.

...

High ceilings and dark wood furniture decorated the master suite. In the center of the room, writhing on a beautiful canopied bed, Mother screamed.

A young Markus cringed and huddled closer to Malcolm's back. The doctor hunched over the bed as the guards held Mother down. Malcolm looked down at Markus in disgust. Then he turned to face Father, standing beside the bed, dressed in his finest business suit. Guards flanked him at both sides.

After a moment, the doctor rose, a bloodied bundle in his arms. Father cradled the small baby in his hands. His face lit up with a joy the boys had never seen before. Malcolm's steady stance faltered. Markus cringed again.

With dark curls and vibrant eyes, the child radiated with light. But the pride on Father's face shifted. He frowned in confusion. Then in anger. Then fear.

Both boys turned to the bed as Father placed the radiant child back into Mother's arms. With thoughtful strides, he crossed the room. At the door, he paused. Sighed.

"Kill them both," he ordered quietly. Then he strolled from the room, shutting the door behind him.

The boys froze.

"No!" Mother cried out. One of the guards snatched the baby from her arms. She lunged after him but the wounds of childbirth restrained her. A second guard walked mindlessly to the lace-covered bassinet beside her bed. He lifted from it another baby, her dark curls and bright eyes identical to her sister's. But there was no radiant glow like her twin.

"Please!" begged Mother from the tangles of her bloody sheets. "Only the second is a threat! That's what he said. The other has no power, no power at all. The second took everything that should have

been split between them. Please, let me keep the first. She's just a baby!"

The guards ignored her.

The boys relaxed with relief as the twins were removed. Mother cried out in anguish.

...

Twins.

I had been a twin. Had I really retained all the supernatural power of my sister in the womb? Was that why I was so powerful?

Even at the moment of my birth, Father had ordered my death. And now I knew why. I was more powerful than I ever imagined. So powerful that energy had literally shone out of me. No wonder they'd tried so hard to kill me. They couldn't take the risk that one day I'd be strong enough to destroy them.

That also explained the beatings and the experiments. I always thought the pain I'd been forced to endure was because Father had tried so hard to kill me and failed. But maybe it was more than that. If they knew I couldn't be killed, Father needed a way to stifle my powers. And he'd found it, with pain and humiliation and constant, unending fear. Anytime I'd lost control of my powers or used them to resist or fight back, the punishments had been so much worse, the pain truly unbearable.

All the new things I'd been doing lately—was something inside me changing, or just waking up? Was there even more inside me that I hadn't discovered yet?

I thought of Theo and immediately knew the answer. Hell, yes, there was more inside me. The question was, how much more?

CHAPTER 38

Markus's mind struggled as memories pushed at him. He fought to stay in the here and now.

"You haven't contacted Father," I said slowly. "We've infiltrated the estate and killed family guards. Why aren't the rest of the guards charging in? Where is Malcolm?"

"I am the more powerful one!" he shrieked. The barn lights shattered around us. I shielded the others from his outburst with my powers. "*I* will be the one to eliminate our enemies. I will destroy the Network, and no one will ever hinder our family's conquests again!" Markus's fists raised high above his head as if in victory.

Wow. His delusions really knew no bounds.

"You honestly believe that by turning over their leader, you can defeat the Network? Or that Father will even care?"

"Not their leader," Markus replied. "The entire Network! The scarred traitor told me about the directory, the psychic *l'annuaire* that held the secrets of all the Network members. I would lay them to waste with the powers I've acquired. Powers that *you* can only dream about. And when I hand their leader to our father, I'll reap the rewards!"

Riiiiight.

"It will prove nothing," I said, but something in his words nagged at me. Acquired powers? We couldn't *acquire* new powers. Could we?

His smile faded. For a moment, he was appeared confused. But then an evil grin pulled at the corners of his mouth. "You didn't die," he said, almost surprised. "You lived. And now you've returned."

The hairs on the back of my neck trembled. Terror shivered up my spine. Deliberately, I turned squarely to face him, blocking Thirteen and Jon as they inched back toward the others.

"I have *not* returned, Markus."

"Oh, but you have, sister. You're here, right in front of me."

My shoulders leaned forward, my body tensed. "I have not returned, Markus," I repeated. "I will *never* return."

He pondered this for a moment. "You think these *people,*" he hissed the word in disgust, "will help you escape?"

I didn't respond. Markus doubled over in laughter, wiped away a stray tear. Utter joy and decision brightened his face.

"*You* are my proof of superiority," he said. "I'll hand over our enemies—trespassing vigilantes who murdered our employees—and will be rewarded for my ingenuity. Then, when I present them with *you*, the powerful Magnolia, they'll know that Malcolm failed in his attempts to end you." He stared off into space. "They will revere me as the strongest of our line."

I cleared my throat. His gaze snapped back to mine. Power gathered at my fingertips, but I forced nonchalance.

"While I'm all for self-deception as a way of life, there are a couple of problems with your invented reality. First, I will *not* go back. You would have to kill me for that to happen, and we all know that simply isn't in the cards. Second, you are not handing anyone over to Father or Uncle Max. I'm taking these men with me. And third, there is *nothing*, no single thing in existence, that would make our father look at you as anything other than the scared, weaker son." I shrugged. "Such is your life."

Markus's eyes went wide. His energy swept over me, tickling the hairs on my skin. It wasn't painful—he wasn't strong enough for that—but it held anticipation for the moment just ahead. I took a deep breath. Stepped forward.

He raised his hand high. His fingers flexed in the air, curling as if around my throat, choking me.

I rolled my eyes. "Oh, please," I said. Markus smiled.

"Theo!" Jon's scream stopped my heart. "Oh God!"

I spun around. Theo fell against the partition wall. His hands clawed at his throat. He gasped for air. Markus growled triumphantly. "Why, Magnolia, you *do* have a weakness."

Theo writhed again. Our connection came to life with a roar. The power surged, elevating me beyond my previous self. Beyond anything I had experienced so far. At once the room darkened. But there was no red or crimson like when I had tortured Banks.

There was only gold.

My hands curved and transformed instantly; my heartbeat throbbed in time with the room around me. Markus attacked. He leaped from his place on top of the tarped mound, tackling me to the ground. Our combined weight and force sent us sliding across the dirty floor. We flew past Theo's contorting body and crashed into the far partition.

My clawed hands clung to Markus. He held me to the ground. I dug my claws deeper into his shoulders, ready to rip off his arms.

He cried out. In a move so fast I missed it, he reached between our bodies. With a loud tear, he ripped open my shirt.

His focus stuttered at my exposed bra, but he shook it off quickly. He pressed his open palm to my chest, right above my heart. His hand blazed with heat, instantly burning through my flesh. The energy radiated deep into my muscles, melting the tissue and heading for my heart. I screamed.

Images of the autopsied Network members flashed into my mind. The traces of polonium 210, the radioactive residue left on their corpses. *This* was the acquired power that Markus spoke of in his rant—the reason he believed himself so powerful now. A nuclear capability. But how?

I shoved deep into his mind, searching his memories. There it was—Father's latest experiment. Markus had been locked inside a secured room while Father had emitted concentrated polonium into the room's airspace. The polonium hadn't caused any pain or disfigurement like Father had hoped, so the experiment had been abandoned and Father had moved on. It was weeks later that Markus realized the chemicals had mutated inside him, reacting with his telekinesis to create a new power. He'd kept his new radioactive ability secret from the rest of the family.

I doubted even a nuclear explosion could permanently kill me. But I really didn't want to test the theory.

I pulled both hands from Markus's back. Then, angling a sharp talon into each ear, I shoved my bloody claws into the sides of his head. He reared back with a shriek. I was on him instantly, launching us against the stairs.

Our weight and force were too much for the rusted staircase. When we hit, the bolts gave, and the staircase collapsed and shattered in metal shards all around us. I kept a firm straddle on Markus's chest, both hands drilling into his temples.

"He doesn't care for you," Markus wheezed as he shuddered beneath me. "I saw it in his head. He only wants you as Malcolm wanted you, as all the filthy minds wanted you."

The words stabbed me like knives. Much more painful than his pathetic radioactive burn. He had pinpointed my fears. Even more, he'd struck at the connection between Theo and me—the one thing I *couldn't* control.

There was a tremor. Like a violent earthquake. The next moment I was in the air. All lingering pain vanished. I peered around the barn. Saw Theo, still gasping for air, Jon and Thirteen at his side. Saw Shane digging through the partition rubble, searching to help the injured hostages.

And I saw me. On top of Markus, my hands still plunged into either side of his head.

I was outside myself, looking down on the scene from several feet above. I recognized my hair, my torn cloths. But my face, my eyes and hands, were all completely foreign. I was strange, beautiful, ethereal. I was a monster.

My eyes swirled, a glowing mixture of crimson and gold. My hands were brown and leathery, joints protruding and claws stretched long.

I watched as my jaw opened wide. My teeth, pointed and long, were as numerous as a shark's. In an animalistic roar I clamped my jaw down on Markus's throat. When I rose, his jugular rested between my teeth.

My eyes closed. A wave of ecstasy shook me. The taste and power of his blood—metallic and tangy—it was too fulfilling not to savor.

Then I opened my eyes.

CHAPTER 39

The world was empty. Not black—my peripheral vision vibrated with color—but blank. Void. I was back in my own skin, but the world around me still felt separate.

I'd killed my brother. I had killed Markus.

There were murmurs everywhere. Voices, thoughts. White noise. A tattered darkness.

Then I saw him. I saw my brother—fear and rage forever frozen in his features.

Strands of Markus's flesh stuck in between my teeth. The taste of blood and skin coated my mouth and trickled down my throat. As I took stock of this—of what I had done—I had to admit to myself the truth: I…didn't…hate…it.

Panic tightened my chest. I had let the power rise up and transform me, allowed it to show itself with talons and beastly teeth. What was I becoming? Or had I already turned? My eyes shut tight. The murmurs around me cleared into coherent thoughts.

We need to get the hostages to the police. We need to get out of here. Get out of here then *go to the police…*

There will be retribution by the family. There is going to be a war now…

I'm going to be sick! God, she's still holding his throat in her hands…

I looked down. Sure enough, the thick, bloodied tube that had once been Markus's throat rested on my lap. *Oh God.*

I twisted onto my hands and knees as my stomached heaved. Blood and bile pooled around me until I had nothing left. And then I heaved again.

Finally empty, I swallowed hard and blocked out everyone's thoughts. I rose to my feet, legs shaky. Markus's throat fell to the ground with a wet thud. My knees buckled underneath me.

Strong hands caught me at the elbow, steadied me. The warmth of my core told me who it was. *How could he even touch me now?*

"Can you walk?" Theo whispered.

I didn't answer. I couldn't. Not after what I'd just done.

"Mag? Can you hear me?"

My eyes clouded with tears. He didn't ask again. Instead, he guided me through the barn toward the garage entrance. My heart burned with every step. The healing had already begun. But the knitting of the wounds inside me was painful. Each heartbeat a fresh ache.

Blood and bodies littered the barn floor. The tools and fallen weapons that Markus had thrown at me were mixed in with the debris. Someone opened the garage door. The storm outside showered the room, muddying the already dirty floor.

Why open the door? Weren't we risking exposure?

Then I saw. The tarp had fallen from the heap Markus had used as a platform. An old Chevy pickup truck, rusted beyond its years, left abandoned by one of the maintenance crew. Shane was buried under the cab's hood. Jon and Thirteen moved the injured hostages into the truck's bed. Theo lifted me and carried me across the barn, I was so shaken.

The storm helped our cover, and since Markus had disconnected the monitors on the barn, the fight hadn't been picked up by the guard station. But once we were out on the main property, the cameras would see us. We had to be fast. I had to get myself together.

Reluctantly, I shrugged off Theo's hold. I still couldn't look at him. Jon laid the unconscious Network member in the truck bed. He'd straightened her bloody clothes, brushed her hair from her battered face.

Cordele.

A loud sob escaped me. They must have captured her just today. She hadn't even been reported missing yet. Her hair matted, her eyes swollen and crusted with blood, her shirt torn to shreds with thick welts covering the exposed skin. Jon turned from the truck and gripped his own shoulder, where shreds of his shirt were used as a tourniquet.

Shane roared the truck to life. Thirteen came around the rear fender. My chest clenched. I looked away. He had seen what I had done to Markus. I wouldn't blame him if he just left me here.

He stepped right up to me, towering over me. Then he gathered me into his arms. He held my face gently to his massive chest. Ran a hand through my matted hair.

"Shh," he whispered. "It's all over now."

I lost it. Tears began streaming, nose running. I couldn't catch my breath. I sobbed and Thirteen held me. Accepted me. Forgave me.

"We need to move," Jon said softly.

I was suddenly exhausted. I wanted to go home to my little farmhouse. To curl up in my yellow quilt and cheap sheets. I leaned into Thirteen, laid my forehead against his chest. He lifted the hem of his tattered shirt and ran it over my mouth, back and forth.

"Will you be able to mask the truck from detection?" he asked me.

His hand moved to my neck. He was wiping away Markus's blood. I nodded weakly.

"Well, don't mask everyone," Jon interjected. His hand still clutched his shoulder. He leaned against the truck for support. "We want the cameras to capture the hostages and some of us as well, don't we?"

"Yes, of course," Thirteen said.

"If you want, I'll only mask myself." I turned to those lying in the truck. "Should I heal them?" I asked.

"No," Theo said from behind me. "We need their injuries as proof."

I looked at Cordele. Fresh tears welled in my eyes. From my back, Theo took my elbow and guided me away from Thirteen. A hand at my waist, he lifted me into the truck bed with the others. His touch was quick, but there was no hesitation. "Let's get outta here," he called over his shoulder before crawling into the truck bed beside me.

I'm a Kelch. Why do you want me? I'm a monster. You saw what I did to Markus.

He snaked his arm around my shoulders and pulled me against his side. "I got you, Mag," he said, his voice husky, reassuring. "You're OK now."

For the first time since that horrible moment on the couch, I looked Theo in the face. He looked over my body, scanning me from head to toe. Frowning. Then he met my eyes. His gaze softened. There was no disgust, no fear. Only concern. Genuine concern.

The tears came once again. *I'll never understand anything.*

Shane tapped on the cab's back window. "Where am I going?" he shouted.

I was too overwhelmed to speak out loud.

Follow the path from the barn to the east entrance. Stay to the left at every fork and you'll end up right at the gate.

My mind was still shut tight. If he tried to respond with his thoughts, I didn't hear.

The truck pulled out of the barn. Rain poured down on us. I made myself invisible. Theo pulled me in closer, and the connection between us hummed. I knew the moment the cameras picked us up because the guard station went crazy. Shouting orders, making phone calls to the main house. I didn't care. The memory of our intimacy stirred something inside me. Theo inhaled sharply. He turned me toward him and looked me right in the eyes.

Everything will be figured out in time, Mag.

It was my turn to gasp. I was still invisible. My mental blocks were solidly in place. How could he see me? How could he speak to me with his thoughts?

Guards blocked the east gate but Shane just sped up. He rammed the gate as guards leaped out of the way. We huddled low as their gunshots fired wildly around us. Shane peeled out onto the highway. The estate wall flew by as we drove along its length. Shane sped through the storm, but I could still make out every black stone embedded in the layers of white bricks.

I did a double take. On the top the wall's ledge, at the very end of the property, Mallroy stood. He leaned against a low branch, watching through the rain as we drove past. His eyes scanned the truck until he found me. Then he winked.

He can't see me. That's impossible.

But he smiled at me. And waved with his fingertips. Then he jumped down from the wall and disappeared back into the estate's woods. It wasn't an illusion. He knew I was alive.

I lifted my face to the pouring sky. The water soaked my hair and rinsed the blood from my face. I huddled closer to Theo, but it didn't really matter. I'd failed. I'd been discovered.

I'd never really be warm again.

CHAPTER 40

It was near dawn. A wonderful breeze blew through the farmhouse, filling it with scents of cornfields and wet grass. The yellow sheers billowed out from my bedroom window. Should I take them with me? They matched so well with the ones in the great room. And it seemed fitting to leave something of myself behind.

The monitor beeped twice. I sighed. *So much for an easy getaway.*

In the kitchen, I retrieved the last of my whiskey. What the hell, there was time for one more quick drink.

The alarm beeped once more. Heavy footsteps hesitated on the front steps.

...

Shane had driven the rusted truck to the hospital. The estate cameras had captured everyone's image. When they arrived with the injured hostages, the police took names and pictures to match to estate tapes.

I wasn't on the cameras. So rather than remaining invisible for the several hours that followed, I'd opted to come home.

When they'd dropped me off at Jon's car, I'd peeked into his thoughts as he'd handed me his keys. The image in his mind had been revolting: me, fighting with demonlike claws, ripping out Markus's throat with beastly teeth. He had tried to shake the image, but I doubted he ever would. Just before they drove away, I'd looked back at Theo. He'd frowned with worry. His dark chocolate eyes held promises of conversations to come and moments alone.

I'd hoped he would come to the farmhouse that night. But it was Thirteen who stopped by after the hostages were settled. The local law enforcement would now work with the FBI to investigate the Kelch family. The estate had been swarmed with officers before he'd even left the hospital. He'd sounded so eager. Finally they had real evidence—living victims willing to testify against my family.

He should have known better.

The next morning, Senator Maxwell Kelch held an impromptu press conference. His voice shaking, he asked the public for sympathy for the soul of his schizophrenic nephew. Twenty-nine-year-old Markus Kelch, in a deluded state of grandeur, had coerced and killed numerous Kelch employees, including several guards who manned the family's estate. He had kidnapped and tortured innocent people, drugging them with hallucinogens stolen from his father's own company. The drugs made his victims see things that couldn't have possibly happened, made their suffering that much worse. That such atrocities had taken place in his own backyard—tears actually came to his eyes—it was more than any one family could take.

He'd said a prayer on live TV for the victims and their families. Then he had addressed the governor. He'd asked for special recognition for those brave citizens who had so gallantly rescued Markus's hostages. If only they could have saved his nephew, as well—before he'd murdered his accomplices and slit his own throat.

Since Markus had used an abandoned part of the estate—and since the maintenance crew could testify to its years of nonuse—there was no way to lay blame on the rest of the family.

No one had visited me that day.

The morning that followed, I watched a replay of Uncle Max's speech. The monitor beeped twice. My body remained cool. *Still no Theo.* The alarm beeped once more when Heather walked through the door. She looked tired, but her smile was genuine. She paused in the entryway just inside the kitchen, then held her hands up in surrender.

"I come in peace," she chuckled. Then she lowered her hands and sobered. "Are you OK?"

She was so casual. *Maybe Jon hadn't told her all the gory details.*

"Uh, yeah, I'm good," I said.

She stepped into the kitchen and pulled out a chair at the table.

"Mind if I have a drink of that?" she asked, nodding to my whiskey.

"Sure." I took down a glass, added some ice and sour mix, then poured out a respectable drink. I slid the glass to her across the table.

She tipped the drink in my direction then drank the entire thing in a series of gulps.

"So I heard about everything," she started. "David Sasser was one of the hostages you guys rescued. He said that Banks was the one who took him—that's why you didn't feel anything at that building we went to. And Thirteen figures Banks was also with your brother when they set up the bomb at Batalkis's house. It was his lead in the first place." She took a deep breath. "I can't begin to imagine what you're going through right now." She folded her hands on the table. Stared at her fingers. "Jon's gunshot wound was pretty bad. And Charles, Marie, and I just got in last night."

There was an edge of guilt to her voice. She felt bad for not coming to see me sooner. "William Broviak is hidden now," she continued. "Even though everyone agrees that the rest of your family doesn't know about him or *l'annuaire*, Thirteen thought it best for him to relocate. He agreed, so they found him someplace not too isolated. He didn't seem too bothered."

I took a drink and waited.

"So…um…what are you going to do now?" she finally asked.

It occurred to me that certain members of the team would probably think it best if I too relocated to some place not too isolated. Probably not a bad idea.

"I'm not sure," I told her honestly.

It didn't seem appropriate to stay at the farmhouse. Although I couldn't pinpoint why. I was still a member of the Network—Thirteen had made a point to mention it on his earlier visit. But to stay here…it just didn't feel right anymore.

Mallroy knew I was alive. They'd come for me now. But for some reason I just wasn't afraid anymore. There were too many other things to deal with now.

Heather's eyes were on me. I finished off my whiskey.

"You shouldn't go," she said as if reading my mind. "There's no need. We don't know for sure if they'll be looking for you. It's not like you have to just disappear. You're still part of the Network, part of our team. We still need your help."

I smiled at my empty glass. Her sentiment meant more than she could know.

"Thank you," I said. "Really, thank you so much for saying that and for coming here." I spun my empty glass on the table. "I don't know what I'm going to do, Heather. There's just so much I need to figure out now." *Like what the hell am I? How much power do I really have? Will I really be able to control it all?* "How can I help the Network, or be with…anyone," *Theo,* "until I know what's going on with me?"

After a moment, she picked up her glass and tilted it over her mouth, shaking it to get the last drop. Then she stood up and looked around.

"Do you still have my cell phone number?" she asked.

"Yeah, I have it."

"Use it," she said. "Please."

I followed her back down the hall to the door. She walked down the front steps. At the last step, she spun around. She sprinted back to the porch and wrapped her arms around me. It was a fast hug; I didn't even have time to return the gesture or pat her on the back, but it was a hug nonetheless.

And it was wonderful.

…

I'd expected her to be my last visitor. But as the early morning sun streamed through the house, Thirteen strolled in. He leaned against the kitchen wall, crossed his arms over his chest. He was as wide as the doorway.

"You can't leave," he said. "I won't let you."

I smiled.

Without a word, I went back to the bedroom. I took a long look around. The room had been mine for a few moments of my life. I threw my black backpack over my shoulder and returned to the kitchen.

The warmth in Thirteen's eyes softened the severity of his frown. He didn't relax his rigid stance. I had to rest one hand on his folded arms and go up on tiptoes to lay a kiss on his scratchy cheek.

"Don't worry," I said as lightly as possible. "At some point, I'll come back for my curtains."

He placed his giant hand over my small one, held it to his arm. He wouldn't look me in the eye. I gently pulled away and walked out of the house.

It was a beautiful morning for a drive. The wind blew softly, the sun shone brightly, and I had a world of uncertainty on my shoulders.

I made it a whole five miles before my stomach tightened. A warmth stirred inside me. The sunlight glowed a little bit brighter as I rounded the next bend.

I pulled off about ten feet away from where Theo rested against his parked Harley. *God, he was beautiful.* The morning sun lightened his dark, wavy hair and glistened off his tanned skin. Dark sunglasses hid his eyes. His white T-shirt stretched across his broad chest, and his low-riding jeans hung perfectly. I remembered that day on the couch—the feel of him under me, his hands kneading my back. The way his lips had trailed from my ear down my throat...

I wanted to leap from the car and fall into his arms. Instead, I gripped the steering wheel tighter.

He ambled over to the driver's side of the car. Stared down at me behind those dark glasses. I didn't read his mind. I didn't need to. He turned his head to stare into the sunlight.

"You aren't the only one with questions, you know," he said finally.

I couldn't speak. Our connection throbbed, rejoicing at our closeness. He crouched down beside my door. "When will you be back?" he asked. Then he cocked an eyebrow at me. "Because you *will* come back to me, Mag."

I smiled a goofy smile. "Soon," I said. It was all I could manage.

He nodded, not looking goofy at all. For a long minute he just stared at me. My heart sped up. He leaned over and brushed his lips against mine. A soft touch of our mouths.

At least that's how it started. But the pressure grew. My hands reached up to hold his jaw. His fingers tangled in my windblown hair. The connection between us heated and spread until…he pulled back sharply. We were both panting. Gently, he took my hands in his, removed them from his face. He put his forehead to mine and sighed.

Then he turned away.

Without another word, he swaggered back to his motorcycle. He swung a long leg over the silver bike and roared the machine to life. Then he drove off, back toward HQ.

I was still relearning how to breathe when his voice whispered through my mind.

Soon, Mag. Soon.

ACKNOWLEDGMENTS

This being a first book, I could easily acknowledge every English teacher and literary professor I've ever had, in addition to anyone who has ever given me a book to read that allowed me to disappear for an afternoon. I'll keep this shorter than that.

First and foremost, I'd like to thank my incredible agent, Joanna Volpe. Her unwavering patience during the process of getting this book made was truly remarkable and came second only to her constant encouragement. I'd also like to thank Maria Gomez and everyone at 47North. Working with people who really "get" you makes a world of difference. Dianne Drake who first told me I was a writer, my writers' group who keep me on track, and all of the individuals responsible for the Midwest Writers Workshop—many thanks for setting me on the right path.

I would not be able to write a single word without the support of an incredible family. J and R—thank you for not complaining about the numerous "cereal for dinner" nights. Babydoll, you already know. Finally, I'd like to thank my sister, Molly, who eagerly reads every version of every story I write and gives the best opinions ever.

ABOUT THE AUTHOR

Megan Powell was born and raised in the Midwest, where she developed a strange affinity for state fairs and basketball humor. When not writing, she can be found feeding her paranormal romance addiction. *No Peace for the Damned* is her first book.